# The Stalker

Alice Rooster

Copyright © 2024 by Alice Rooster

All rights reserved.

No portion of this book may be reproduced in any form without written permission from the publisher or author, except as permitted by U.S. copyright law.

# Contents

1. Chapter 1- Ryder — 1
2. Chapter 2- Ryder — 5
3. Chapter 3- Hailey — 9
4. Chapter 4- Ryder — 13
5. Chapter 5- Hailey — 17
6. Chapter 6- Ryder — 21
7. Chapter 7- Hailey — 25
8. Chapter 8- Ryder — 29
9. Chapter 9- Hailey — 33
10. Chapter 10- Ryder — 37
11. Chapter 11- Hailey — 41
12. Chapter 12- Ryder — 45
13. Chapter 13- Hailey — 49
14. Chapter 14- Ryder — 53
15. Chapter 15- Hailey — 57

16. Chapter 16- Ryder     61

17. Chapter 17- Hailey     65

18. Chapter 18- Ryder     69

19. Chapter 19- Hailey     73

20. Chapter 20- Ryder     78

21. Chapter 21- Hailey     82

22. Chaper 22- Ryder     86

23. Chapter 23- Hailey     91

24. Chapter 24- Ryder     95

25. Chapter 25- Hailey     99

26. Chapter 26- Ryder     104

27. Chapter 27- Hailey     108

28. Chapter 28- Ryder     112

29. Chapter 29- Hailey     117

30. Chapter 30- Ryder     122

31. Chapter 31- Hailey     126

32. Chapter 32- Ryder     131

33. Chapter 33- Hailey     136

34. Chapter 34- Ryder     141

35. Chapter 35- Hailey     146

# Chapter 1- Ryder

M y eyes memorize her every move as she roams around her home.

I will never fucking get sick of this.

I shouldn't be doing this to her, she's much too good for me. But even the thought of not seeing her smooth skin, her soft hair, her perfect self.... It's absolute torture. But I've never been a good man.

I need to watch her, protect her from anyone who would try take advantage of her. I will never let anything or anyone hurt my perfect girl. Nobody will harm a hair on her god damn head.

I watch as she curls up on the couch, wrapping a plush blanket around her skin. I smile to myself as she nuzzles her face into the softness of the blanket, imagining her snuggling into my chest.

I wasn't always like this, obsessive.

I couldn't help myself though, the second my eyes landed on her I felt drawn to this woman like never before in my life. I remember it perfectly, walking into the bar and seeing her beautiful self behind the counter. She was running around pouring drinks for the crowded bar, yet she carried herself with such fucking grace. Then, as if I wasn't already loosing my sanity at the sight of her, she flipped some creep off that was hitting on her, telling him to "fuck off". I've never smiled so hard in my life.

I'm not shy in the slightest, had no problems getting women's attention either but she made me speechless. That's what led me here.

It started small, watching over her at work, making sure she got home safe....But then it developed into an addiction, I needed more. I craved her every second of the day.

Now I watch her. Protect her. Waiting for the right moment. I don't want to scare her off, but fuck I could never let her go. I had to do this perfectly.

I had experience with this kind of shit, stalking someone.

Had to for some old jobs I did, I didn't like it then but damn I'm fucking enjoying it now.

I'm a bounty hunter, not that I like hunting down people, but it makes good money. It's what I'm good at.

Damn I'd chase this pretty girl to the ends of the earth though.

Hailey fucking Weber. She'll be the death of me I swear. She laughs softly at the movie she's watching, and god I wish I was close enough to hear the sweet sound. The sun begins to set, causing deep pinks and oranges to fill the sky. Once the movie is over, she comes over to the window to see for herself.

I make sure I'm hidden in the trees behind her house as she looks out. I can't help but peer up at her, unable to resist looking at her pretty fucking face as she smiles at the sky.

Eventually, she backs away from the window, moving to her bedroom. She begins stripping out of her clothes from work as she makes her way to her bathroom.

I sigh softly as her bathroom door shuts, hiding her pretty self from me. I can only imagine what she looks like naked... water cascading down her soft skin... lathering soap over her soft curves...Fuck.I wait patiently for her to come back out, my eyes trained on her bedroom window. I have a fucking problem.

I've been watching her for about 2 months now, my obsession growing every single day. She's stunning, tall, strong... she has these deep brown curls that form into soft ringlets, dark blue eyes, and a smirk that would bring me to my knees quite literally. She's too good for me, I think that's obvious to anyone. But fuck if I'm way too selfish to let her go... I never will.

I perk up as she exits the steamy bathroom. Her curls are pulled up into a bun on the top of her head, a few wet strands sticking to her face. She has just a towel wrapped around her body, barely reaching the tops of her thighs. What I wouldn't give to have them wrapped around my fucking face...

I greedily take in as she rubs her body with coconut scented lotion. I can almost smell it, fuck. Her legs are long, with thicker thighs that are genuinely my own personal heaven. Her skin glistens as the lotion soaks into her skin, and my dick twitches at the sight.

She returns to the bathroom, slipping on her pajamas. She comes back out in little black shorts and an oversized t shirt, lying back in bed.

She curls up under the sheets, turning the lamp next to her bed off as the room goes dark. I slip out of the trees as my view of her goes away.

I need more.

I go to her back door, taking the spare key I made and quietly unlocking it. I leave my shoes outside to avoid leaving any trace of me behind.

Silently, I shut the door behind me as I make my way over to her couch first. I sit down on the soft cushions, bringing the blanket she used to my face, inhaling her subtle sweet coconut scent.

I go around the room, observing anything new before I make my way to her bedroom. Peaking in through the door, I watch her chest rise and fall slowly with her breathing, telling me she's asleep.

I step in the room quietly, not wanting to disturb my pretty girl's sleep. The moonlight from the window is just enough for me to make out her face, and the outline of her body beneath the covers.

I can smell the lingering scent of coconut from her shower, and a grin makes its way to my face. I come closer to her bed, hearing the soft sound of her peaceful breathing. She looks like a fucking angel. So perfect. Gently, I reach down and ever so softly brush a piece of hair away from her soft cheek.

My perfect girl.

# Chapter 2- Ryder

I stepped into the bar where she worked around 6. She just started her shift about 20 minutes ago and I grin as I see her come out behind the bar. So fucking gorgeous.

She's wearing some black jeans that fit her way too fucking good, and a black tank top that gives me a peak of her cleavage.I make my way to a secluded booth, sitting back before the bar becomes busy. The top half of her curls are pulled out of her face with a clip behind her head, a few strands falling out and brushing against her cheekbones as she works.

I come in here pretty regularly now, but try to keep a low profile, not wanting her to get suspicious just yet.I go over and order a drink from her sometimes, but never am able to start a conversation. It's like my brain looses its composure talking to her and I feel like a damn idiot.

I have to fight to hold myself back whenever she gets hit on or someone is rude to her.She doesn't fucking deserve that.My beautiful girl only deserves the best, someone to take care of her. Me.

The bar begins to fill up slowly as it grows later and she remains focused on taking orders and making drinks. I smile as she blows a strand of hair out of her face as she pours another glass. Her cheeks are becoming rosy from running around all night. She'd look so good all flushed and beneath me...I take a breath, collecting myself as I watch her work.

I wonder if she liked her job? If she was with me she wouldn't have to work if she didn't want to....I smile to myself... Soon.

A few rowdy college guys bust through the doors laughing and yelling. I sit back, annoyed with their obnoxious behavior. I make sure to keep my eyes on them as they go over to the bar, calling over my girl to come take their order. Fucking pricks.

I can tell as she sighs annoyed, forcing a smile as she walks over to take their orders. My grip on my table tightened as I see them all looking over her, not even trying to be subtle as they stare down her tank top. They spit out some stupid drink orders, and one of the boys adds:

"And I'll take your number too sweetheart" with a cocky grin.

My fingers itch for my gun. I fucking swear. She gets hit on often, but it's egotistical assholes like these that set me off.

"No thanks" my pretty girl says as she moves to walk away. Good girl. The kid doesn't seem to understand the fucking word "no", as he goes and wraps grubby hand around her arm, not letting my girl leave.

"Come on sugar" the boy grins, gripping her arm.

I'm out of my fucking chair.

Before I even get there, Hailey elbows the dude so that he releases her, muttering "fuck you" before turning away. Good fucking girl.

Before the douchebag can say another word I put my arm around him and him and his friends turn to look at me now. They gulp softly. Good.

"Let's get some air boys" I say lowly before subtly dragging them outside the bar. Away from my precious girl.

"You must really think you're the shit huh? You think you can put your hands on a woman huh?" I ask the guy who grabbed my girl.

He looks up at me with widened eyes,"Man- I didn't do shit just chill out-" Before he can finish spitting out nonsense I punch him square in the face. He groans as blood pours from his nose. I push him back into the arms of his scared friends.Fucking pussies.

"Don't let me see any of you again. Leave." I tell them, fighting the urge to smirk as they scurry away.

I make my way back inside and take a seat at the bar. After making a few more drinks, my girl comes over to me with a soft smile. God she's so fucking good.

"What happened with those guys huh?" She asks me sweetly.Her voice sounds like honey

I look up at her for a moment before collecting myself and answering:"Suggested they head home" I tell her, trying to hide my smirk.She raises an eyebrow at me for a moment as if she knows I'm lying but leaves it alone.

"Can I get you something?""A Jack and coke please" I tell her with a grin.She nods softly, walking off. In a few minutes, she hands me my drink, and I thank her before she runs off to make some more orders.I sip my drink slowly, savoring it as I watch her work seamlessly.

More hair has fallen out of her clip as the night has gone on, her curls messy but stunning.I can't help but watch her the whole night, time seeming to slip by before I realize it.

It's last call by the time I recognize how long I've been here. I've been distracted.

She doesn't seem to even notice my presence as she cleans up the bar, getting ready to close. I place a fifty on the table for her before getting up. As I'm leaving, I see her come out with her things ready to go. Just fucking do something. "You want me to walk you to your car or something? It's late..." I say, turning back to face her. I let out a silent breath of relief as she smiles softly and tells me, "Yeah, thanks"

I try and hide my massive grin as I hold the door open for her, following her back to her car. The walk is quiet but peaceful, and ends way too soon for my liking. She looks up at me with a smile, "Thank you" she says again sweetly before getting into her car. "Anytime" I tell her, backing off as she drives away. Anytime doll.

# Chapter 3- Hailey

I could tell it was him the second he walked through the front door of the bar. I didn't even have to look up. This massive fucking idiot... i smiled to myself.

He sits down in a corner booth trying to not draw any attention. But how the hell does he think I'm not going to notice his 6'4 ass walk through the bar. It's honestly hilarious.

I've had a stalker for months now... and I just know it's him. At first it bothered me. I was scared, felt like my privacy was invaded.

But after some time, I realized the man had no intentions of hurting me. I could feel in my bones when his eyes were on me, staring into my soul. I began to welcome the feeling. It almost felt flattering in a way, to have someone be so deeply infatuated with you.

I know that he follows me home from work, and makes sure I make it there safely. It's reassuring sometimes, having someone protecting you.

Even figured out exactly where he hides behind the trees of my place... and I'm too observant to miss his large frame in the shadows. He's not very good at this...

It's getting hard to keep my face impassive at this point, especially when he speaks to me. I almost want to laugh at the way this massive man can't even ask me on a date... it's kind of adorable aside from the fact he looks like he could tear someone apart.

When I say massive, I mean he is truly massive. I'm quite tall and he stands a good 6 inches taller than me. I have to look up to meet his eyes when he's standing.I love that shit.

He's clearly very strong, his large muscles visible even under his heavy jacket.His hair is dark, and he has pretty hazel eyes that light up when he sees me. I can see light scars on his hands and face, they look good on him. Make him look even more intimidating.

I pretend to not notice as he drags those college pricks outside, biting my lip as I see him punch the shit out of the one who put his hands on me.Hot.I act unaware when he comes back inside and sits at the bar.Perfect. I love this part.

He doesn't always come up and get a drink from me. Sometimes he just watches. I can just feel his eyes on my the entire time, and I have to resist the urge to look back at him.

When I ask him what happened to those guys he merely tells me "Suggested they went home"I smirk slightly at the answer, knowing better.God his voice is hot. Deep.

I don't ask anything further, leaving him to go make his drink. I purposely bend over slowly with my back to him, giving him a nice view of my ass as I grab a bottle from below the bar.What? A girl can't have some fun too?

I smirk internally as I feel his gaze burning into my skin before I turn around, giving him his drink with a smile.He sips on the drink the rest of the night.

I've noticed he never gets more than a drink, maybe two, but his eyes never leave me the whole night. I act fucking oblivious.

After last call, I notice a 50 on the bar from him, pocketing it quickly before grabbing my things. He always pays me way over what he owes me. I used to be shocked at first, but now it's normal for me.

I see him lingering at the exit as I come out. Adorable.

He never says much to me besides a quick drink order so when I hear his voice, it catches me off guard a bit. "You want me to walk you to your car or something? It's late..." he says, almost in a nervous tone.

Fuck yes I do. I tell him yes, trying to hide the fucking smile on my face as he walks right beside me to my car. I have to hold in my laugh until I'm pulling out of the parking lot.

I can easily handle myself but who am I to say no to him when he asks so sweetly...

After a few minutes, I look in my rear view mirror seeing the familiar blacked out dodge charger following about a block behind. Right on time.

I wonder if he's done this before... he's not very good at keeping a low profile. I laughI pull into my driveway. My house is fairly secluded just outside the city, surrounded by forest in the back. I don't see the car anymore, but I know he'll be here soon. He always is.

I make my way inside, opening up the curtains before heading to the kitchen to make myself some dinner. Gotta give him a good view...I turn on some music before making myself some pasta. I'm starving.

I let my hips sway to the music as I move around the kitchen, chopping up an onion. I begin making the sauce as the pasta boils.

Then I feel his eyes on me. It makes my heart stop for a moment every single time.I don't have to look out the window anymore to know he's there. I can feel it.

I smile to myself as I move my hips to the music, stirring the sauce occasionally. Once I'm finished, I put some of the pasta in a bowl, digging into it as I sit in a loveseat I have placed my the window.I put on a show in the background but I can barely pay attention to it, knowing he's watching.

Eventually, my exhaustion from the day hits me as I get up to go to bed. I make sure I lock the doors before heading upstairs.Gotta make him work for it a little bit. Come on.

I head to the bathroom before slipping on some sweatpants and a tank top, getting into my bed. I can feel his gaze on me until I finally turn off the lights. I wonder if he'll come in tonight...

# Chapter 4- Ryder

Fuck, she has no idea what she's doing to me.

Moving her hips like that while she goes around the kitchen.

I could be cooking for her... taking care of her. I watch as she eats with a smile, happy to see her get a good meal in after a long shift. I notice her get up, yawning and stretching her arms over her head in the most adorable way. My pretty girl is tired

I move to get a better view through her bedroom window as she comes out of her bathroom in a pair of blue sweatpants and a white tank top that makes it clear she's not wearing a bra. Damn.

I frown slightly as the lights turn off and I can no longer see her. I know I should go home. I've been being much to risky lately going inside her house...But fuck if I can't stop myself. I need her. I use my key to silently open her back door.

Creeping inside, I can smell the pasta she made earlier. Fucking delicious. What I wouldn't do for a taste of something she made...I move past the thought as I make my way upstairs.

One of the floorboards creak beneath my weight and I pause for a few moments, listening for any sign of movement. Once I hear nothing, I proceed to her bedroom. The door is slightly ajar as I peak inside; seeing my perfect girl fast asleep.Such a deep sleeper I smile to myself.

My heart beats faster as I look over her dimly lit face, her curls sprawled out messily over the pillow.

One of her thighs slips out from beneath the blankets and I can't help the urge to feel her perfect skin.My fingers trace over her gently, her skin feeling like silk against my roughness.I have to fight to keep myself from letting out a groan at the sensation.She's so perfect. Fucking made for me.I just know it.

I move around to the other side of the bed, looking over the smooth muscles of her back as I sit down on the edge of the bed softly.She shifts ever so slightly but then drifts back into a peaceful sleep.Such a deep sleeper... has no fucking idea

My fingers move on their own to her silky hair lying on the pillow. I gently wrap one of the ringlets around my finger before letting it fall back down onto the pillow.

I do the same thing over and over, playing with her pretty hair as she sleeps like an angel.I go to her bathroom, taking a little bit or her hair oil in my hands before coming back to her.

I run my fingers through her locks ever so gently, making sure to work the oil into each strand.My pretty doll was too tired to do this herself tonight... I'll take care of her though.

Once I'm satisfied, I lean down, taking a deep inhale into her hair, sighing softly at the scent.I brush her hair away from her face as I lean down, pressing a soft kiss into the crook of her neck.Her skin feels fucking perfect against my lips. I'd kiss every single inch of her if I could.

I stand up slowly, walking around her room for a little while, observing everything. I see her work clothes sprawled on the floor, and I reach for her shirt and lift it to my nose. Coconuts. She always smells like coconuts. I then move to her dresser, opening the top drawer where her panties are.

I carefully look through them, trying not to rearrange everything as I go through and pick one out. I take one of the pairs that I find, a black lacy thong that would look fucking perfect against her skin.

I slide it into the pocket of my jeans, smiling that I'll have a piece of her to hold onto. I look back at her sleeping face, sighing as I know I won't be able to see her for a little while. I hate leaving her.

But I have a job to do tomorrow and I'll be gone for a day or two. As much as I hate having to leave her for even a day, I still have to do some occasional jobs here and there. I need to make sure I have plenty of money to spoil my girl when she's finally mine. Anything my pretty girl wants, she'll have.

I sadly force myself to step away from my sleeping angel as I leave her room. Making my way back downstairs, I slip out the door I came in. Of course I make sure to lock the door behind me, ensuring everything is how she left it.

Grabbing my bag from my car, I place a few security cameras around the outside of her house. They're small enough for her not to ever notice, but they'll give me some peace of mind while I'm gone, ensuring nothing happens to her.

Once I'm satisfied, I check my phone to make sure I have a good view from the cameras. Perfect.

I frown as I walk away from her home, wanting nothing more than to watch over her through the night. But I have important things to do. I make my way back to my car, heading to my apartment and packing a few things I'll need before going on my job. I want to get this shit over as soon as possible.

I head off to pick up an unmarked truck and load it up with my equipment before heading out. I'm off to a city about 2 hours away from here, and it pains me to be so far away from her.

But I'm doing this for her, I remind myself. I drive by her house one last time before heading off. I'll be back soon pretty girl.

# Chapter 5 - Hailey

He was here last night. I know it. I really am a deep sleeper, I'm not faking any of that, but I can smell him on my sheets. Just faintly. But it smells good. So good.

When I get up, I go and stretch out my limbs over by the window. When I don't feel his eyes on me I realized he left already.

I sigh, making my way downstairs. I make myself some coffee, and relax on the kitchen counter.

He doesn't always stay around and watch me but it's getting rare that I'm left alone nowadays so I try to enjoy it. Grabbing a slice of banana bread for breakfast, I decide to head off to the gym.

I head upstairs to get changed into a black sports bra and some matching leggings before I get in my car to leave. Black is my favorite color. I have a feeling he likes it too...

Once I make it there, I go over to the corner and do some stretching before I make it to the weight room. I do a quick scan of the people who are there, wondering if I'll see him.

He occasionally comes in to watch me. Always has his hood up and just stares at me while sitting on some machine near the back.

As if having your hood up is going to hide your massive fucking self...

I'm slightly disappointed when I can't find his large frame anywhere, but move on with my workout. After a while, I've worked up quite a sweat, my skin glistening as I catch my breath.

I notice some guy behind me eyeing up and down and I cringe internally. It's not the same. I smile thinking about what my stalker would do to him if he was here.

After another hour or so, I finish up my workout, heading to the grocery store to pick up a few things before I make my way back home.

I spend some time cleaning up my place and putting everything away since I don't have work tonight.

After I've finished up cleaning, satisfied with my now organized home, I make my way upstairs. I head into my bathroom, stripping out of my clothes before starting a bath.

I put some epsom salts and oils into to tub, inhaling the warm fragrance that comes from the water. Letting out a sigh, I slip into the bath, allowing the heat to sooth my sore muscles from the gym. I take in a deep breath, relaxing and closing my eyes. Nearly an hour goes by as I try and relax, the water eventually running cold.

Stepping put of the water, I wrap a towel around myself before i do my skincare. I apply some coconut lotion to my body, massaging it into my skin gently. I then take my hair down, putting some oil in it before I throw it into a quick bun.

Finally I step back out of my room, looking over at the window for a moment as I still don't feel him watching me. Strange.

I brush it off before getting changed into some comfortable shorts and a sweatshirt, making my way downstairs. I sit back in the loveseat by the window, grabbing a book to read for a while until he shows up. The sky begins to get darker after a few hours, and my stomach starts to rumble.

I sigh, looking at the clock, seeing it's nearly 7pm. I get up, walking over to the kitchen to make myself some food. It almost feels unnatural to be here without him watching me. There have been times where he goes off for a few hours, or part of the day, but this long was abnormal.

I told myself to just enjoy the privacy for once and have a normal night. I made myself dinner, chopping up some asparagus to roast in the oven with some chicken. I wait as it cooks on the kitchen counter, kicking my feet impatiently. This just feels so boring without him.

Once the food is finished, I sit down on the couch and turn on a movie. I put on a comedy to get me in a better mood as I ate.

•••

As the movie ended, I got up to put away the dishes I used before walking over to the window. The sky was nearly dark down. He still isn't here. He's always here before I go to sleep...

My eyes search the darkness for something but I find nothing. I begin to get worriedI know, fucking worried about my stalker. What the fuck am I doing.

I make my way upstairs and lie back in my bed. I stay up later than usual, keeping my light on so that he can see me if he shows up. Around midnight, I settle back in bed, realizing he's not coming. I should be glad.

I turn off the lamp beside my bed and slip underneath the covers. As I try and fall asleep I find myself getting restless.It feels like I'm missing something.I keep worrying, and shut my eyes to try and force myself to drift off. it doesn't work. It's almost like I feel vulnerable.

I know that makes no sense because for the first time in weeks, there's not someone watching me, but I can't help it.I feel like there's nobody out there to protect me, make sure I'm safe through the night. I toss and turn for hours until eventually my body succumbs to exhaustion.

I sleep in late the next day. Well into the afternoon. I never do that.When I finally do get out of bed, I find myself walking over to the window, hoping to feel the warmth of his eyes on me.Nothing.

Absolutely nothing.I walk around my home, looking for any signs he was here while I was sleeping.Nothing.

I pace around my home, feeling anxious. What happened? Did he loose interest? Did he find someone else to watch over? I fucking feel insane when the thought of that makes me feel jealous.Where the fuck did he go?

# Chapter 6- Ryder

I'm here staking out the motel this guy is supposedly in, haven't gotten a sighting of him yet.I glance down at my phone with a smile as I see my girl coming home from the gym in a workout set that fits her too fucking good.

Her curls are messy and falling around her face as she brings in groceries from the car.So fucking pretty

I fucking hate this.Not being able to see her in person. Not being able to touch her, smell her. Fuck.

This job is taking longer than I'd like and it's pissing me the fuck off.But I'm not about to do anything stupid. I can't mess this shit up and not be able to come back to her.I need to be patient.

It grows dark outside and I still have yet to see any movement or sign from my target. I'm exhausted. I've been watching this motel for nearly 8 hours. I used to not mind this, the waiting. It was peaceful.

But now all I can think about is every minute that goes by that keeps me away from my girl.I don't see her come back outside her house the rest of the night, and I know she doesn't have work.Good. She's safe there with me watching her.

After midnight, I shut my eyes to sleep for a few hours, knowing Hailey is safe and sleeping in her bed.I wake up to my alarm around 4am, groaning softly. The first thing I do is check the cameras around her house to make sure nothing looks disturbed.Everything looks good. I let out a small sigh of relief.

I take the pair of panties I stole from her out of my pocket, feeling the silky fabric in my fingers. She'd look so fucking good in these.I smile down at the wad of fabric, the feeling of it calming me down as I look up at the target's room.Another day.

I'm eating some food I packed when I see movement on the cameras outside Hailey's house. She walks outside to her car wearing a pair of black leggings and a black long sleeve shirt.

Her hair is pulled out of her face into a ponytail.She looks tired.I frown as I look closer at her faceDid something happen?Did she not sleep?Have a nightmare?Fuck.

I watch as she gets into her car and drives off, wishing I was there to make sure she got to work safely.I don't like her driving when she's this tired.

I sigh, running my hands down my face as my anxiousness builds.I keep an eye on the motel as I take my computer out, finding a way into the security camera system for her work.Just to keep an eye on her.

I'm relieved as I see her car pull into the parking lot safely, watching as she makes it into the bar.She sets up for the night, cutting up limes and restocking bottles.

I make sure to glance over at my computer every few moments once people start coming in. After a few hours, I notice her head keeps popping up with every person that walks through the doors. She's distracted, like she's waiting for someone.Who are you waiting for doll?

I try not to let my thoughts get out of hand, but the idea that she's waiting for someone, maybe a man...Fuck. I hope I'm wrong.

I grumble as i continue watching the target, waiting for any sign so i can make I move.I just need to get back to my girl.

She looks exhausted, moving slower tonight. She doesn't smile at her regulars like she usually does. Doesn't talk to anyone more than necessary. I don't like it. It's not her.

What's troubling you love?Is it the person you're waiting for?He doesn't fucking deserve you. You're too perfect. All mine.

This is taking longer than I planned.I'm fucking itching to get back to her. She's my addiction, and fuck I'm going through withdrawal.

I just want to feel her smooth skin, smell her coconut scent. Anything.But I need to be patient for her. For us.

I watch her work through the night, up until last call. I noticed her sad face as she gathers her things and walks out of the bar. My fucking gut hurts at her face. Makes me want to punch something.

I just want to kiss her pretty face over and over again until she's forced to smile.God she has a pretty fucking smile.It's a rare sight, but I adore when she smiles so big her teeth show, causing little dimples to form on either side of her rosy lips. My fucking favorite sight in the world.

I watch to make sure she arrives home safe, seeing her tired body move inside.I'll be there soon doll. I'll play with your hair and tell you all my favorite things about you while I make sure you sleep peacefully.

Knowing she's home for the night, I return my attention back to the motel as I wait more excruciatingly slow hours with nothing to see. I eventually allow myself to sleep for an hour or two, getting back up before the sun rises.

I wait, so fucking close to giving up and running back to my girl. I need her. So fucking badly. It's around 11am when my eye catches something in the window. A shadow. Something.

I stay on high alert as a woman approaches his door about 30 minutes later in a tiny dress. A hooker. Fucking prick. When he opens the door slightly, I get sight of him. Fucking finally. I'm not waiting another second to get my hands on this slimy son of a bitch.

I grin as I make my way up to the door, kicking my way in. There's no cameras here so I'm not worried.

The woman looks shocked and I motion to the the door for her to leave and she runs away. The man takes the same opportunity, trying to bolt. "Not a fucking chance"

I drag his squirming body to the bathroom, making this as quick as possible. Can't wait to kill this disgusting fucker who kept me from my woman.

I hold him down before putting a bullet in the back of his head. He slumps down into the tub, and I quickly leave, calling a team to clean this up. I have more important things to get to. I grin, hopping in my car.

# Chapter 7- Hailey

I force myself out of bed to get ready for work. I throw on the first things I can find, putting my hair up into a ponytail. I'm too fucking tired to try and look good.

I get to work, setting up the bar for tonight. Maybe he'll come to my shift tonight? He's usually here when I'm working.

The thought keeps me going through the night, making drinks and dealing with customers. I can't help but look up every time the door opens, wondering if it's him. It's not.

My disappointment and tiredness only grows through the night, and I feel like falling asleep right on the floor by last call. I grudgingly grab my things, closing up for the night as I walk back to my car. Alone.

I thank god I didn't somehow crash my car on the way home, I'm not even sure I was conscious the whole time. I drag myself inside, peering out the window one last time before falling back in bed. My eyes fall closed on their own and I'm out within minutes.

I toss and turn all night, feeling cold and anxious. I keep waking up every few hours, looking around before forcing myself back to sleep. I hate this feeling. I don't even know why I'm feeling this way. Fuck.

I wake up to the bright sun the next morning, groaning and rolling out of bed. I feel terrible. Sick. I go to the bathroom to look in the mirror. I fucking look awful too.

I don't even bother to look out the window as I get undressed from my work clothes that I slept in. I turn the shower on, letting the water get steaming hot before stepping in. Taking in a deep breath, I let the hot water hit my skin. I lean my head back, soaking my tangled curls.

After rinsing out my hair, I lather myself with coconut body wash, the scent calming me down. I let the water run down over me, just sitting with myself before washing my hair.

When I step out, it takes me a while to detangle it before putting some product in. I step back into my room, throwing on some black jeans and a t shirt.

I eventually make my way downstairs, finding something quick to eat for lunch. I just don't have the energy to make anything. I feel so fucking lonely.

I'm always alone, I know that. I'm not crazy. Nothing has really changed, but for whatever reason it didn't feel so lonely when I knew he was watching me. Someone was there.

I let my curls stay down today as I gather my things for work, knowing I'd have to leave soon. I need to move on with my life. Get over this stupid bullshit.

Once it hits 3pm, I make my way to my car, getting in. I park in my usual spot, heading inside before setting up like always. About an hour into my shift, I hear the door open harshly, my eyes looking up at the noise.

It's him.My eyes widen for a moment.

I notice he's breathing heavily, his chest rising and falling quickly as I feel the warmth of his eyes studying every inch of me. I can't even help the smile that comes to my face.He's here.

I have to turn around for a moment to compose myself before getting back to work. I keep secretly taking glances up at him as he sits in a corner booth, watching me quietly.I feel fucking alive again, light on my feet.

I notice he seems different today. Not as composed. He came in here so chaotically, it almost made me laugh.

But he also looks tired, like he's been up for days. He has a slight stubble on his face and I can't say I hate it.It suits him.

I can't help but be curious what happened, why he disappeared.If he's okay.But I'm also annoyed.

I don't have a right to be really, but I was pissed that he left with no warning.I felt fucking horrible, worried, confused, jealous. I haven't felt those things in a long time.

So I tried not to give him any attention. I let him just sit there and watch. I wanted tot see if he'd do anything. If he'd come over.Eventually, it worked.

He sits down at the bar, looking over at me with a soft grin."A Jack and coke please" he says smoothly Fuck, his voice gives me goosebumps.

I give him a nod and a smile, for some reason my voice failing me at the moment."Thanks doll" he says softly, and I barely catch it.Fuck.That's sounds way too good. Good enough to make my knees fucking weak.

But I have to remind myself I'm mad at him.So I just continue on, making his drink without a word.He just keeps looking at me with that stupid smile on his face.Looking so fucking pleased with himself.Cocky motherfucker.

I hand him his drink, trying to ignore his presence through the rest of the shift. It's hard though.He's hard to ignore even as a stranger. Fucking massive idiot.

As the night gets later, most people clear out of the bar, and I start cleaning up.He's still here though.And I hate that that gives me butterflies.

As I grab my things I notice he's waiting by the exit. I meet his eyes finally.

"Walk you to your car?" He asks simplyI nod softly.The walk is silent but comfortable. He's so fucking close to me I can smell him. The same scent that was left on my bed a few days ago.

He opens my car door for me.A stalker who's a fucking gentlemen. Cute.

I say a quick thank you, and he smiles at the sound of my voice.He just nods and waits for me to pull away.It isn't till I'm out of the parking lot that he turns around, going back to his car.

I rush home, eager to see what happens tonight.Soon after I'm inside, I grab some ice cream from the freezer. Curling up on the couch while I put on a show.

About 10 minutes later, I can feel it.His eyes on me.I smile to myself, indulging in the familiar warmth.Soon after, I think of a plan. I wanted to push him. Make him regret leaving me.

I make my way upstairs to my bedroom, and before doing anything I walk over to my window, and close the curtains. I smirk to myself.If you're going to leave me, you don't deserve to watch me.... plus I want to see what he'll do.

# Chapter 8- Ryder

Everything just became so much better when I finally set my eyes on her. I got there as quickly as I could, practically running into the door on my way in.

Her pretty blue eyes snapped to mine as I came in the door. They widened a bit in surprise. She's never done that before. But I also probably came in here like a crazed man.

I couldn't stop fucking smiling. My eyes couldn't stay off her for a second. My perfect fucking girl. She looked better now, happier. Awake.

I was worried about her. She seemed so dull and tired over the cameras, but now, to see her smile, her perfect fucking smile, everything was right again. I made my way to the bar, ordering a drink with her. She seemed a little flustered, but I think it's from her lack of sleep.

I didn't miss the way her thighs clenched ever so slightly when I called her "doll". Does my pretty girl like that? Good.

I couldn't keep the grin off my face the whole night, and I can only hope I wasn't freaking her out. I gave her a large tip per usual before waiting at the door for her. She walked over to me, her pretty blue eyes meeting mine.

"Walk you to your car?" I asked She gave me a soft nod, and I followed her out to her car.I opened the door for her and I swear I heard her laugh under her breath.Hm...

I watch as she leave before going to follow behind her.

When I got to her place, I made my way to my usual spot, seeing her on her couch with a pint of chocolate ice cream.So fucking adorable.

I can tell she's watching a show, the glow of her tv reflecting off of her pretty face.After a while, she turns off her tv and makes her way to her room.God I missed this. Watching her. My fucking perfect girl.

I hide myself as she walks over to her window.When I look back up, a frown forms on my face.She closed her curtains.

Fuck.Does she know?Is she starting to suspect something?No. No.I've been so careful. I never leave a trace behind. She can't know.

I calm myself, letting go of my worries.But now there's another problem.I can't see her. I need to fix this.I collect myself as I make my way to her back door.

I've never done this while she's awake...I peer inside the house, no sight of her as I quickly unlock her door, slipping inside silently.

I can hear the shower on upstairs. Perfect.I go outside her bedroom door, listening to the water running.I inhale deeply, smelling the sweet coconut scent drifting from her bathroom.

After a few minutes, I hear the water stop and I slip away from the door.She can't see me.I drift back downstairs, deciding I should keep a safe distance till she's asleep.

I'm surprised as I hear her soft feet coming down the stairs. What is she doing?

I find a place to hide myself quickly as I see her go into the kitchen, a smile forming on her face. She grabs a mug, making herself a cup of tea.

As she waits for the water to heat up, she sits up on the kitchen counter. Her long legs dangle off the edge carelessly, as if she has no worries. If only you knew I was here angel.

Once her tea is ready, I hear her go back upstairs, her bedroom door closing behind her. I step out, quietly walking around her place as I wait for her to drift asleep. I pick up a few things around the house, wanting it to be nice for her.

After a while, I make my way up to her room, opening her door as softly as I can. There she is. Fucking gorgeous.

She lays there curled up on her side, underneath a plush blanket. I quietly walk closer, the coconut scent of hers flooding the room. She's only wearing a small tank top and shorts tonight and fuck does she look good. Like she's fucking trying to tempt me.

I walk over to her, sitting softly on the edge of her bed. I brush a few loose curls out of her pretty face, admiring every feature. Her soft skin, long eyelashes, her perfect cheekbones, rosy lips... god.

I run my fingers through her curls softly, careful not to mess up her silky ringlets. She just makes me fucking melt. I just listen to her soft breathing as I graze my fingers over her smooth skin. But then she does something that makes my heart stop.

She hums softly in her sleep, wrapping an arm around my wrist and curling up closer to my touch. Fuck. What a fucking angel. She has no idea what she's doing to me. She has no idea that she's curling up into the touch of a man. A bad man who doesn't deserve her.

Her fucking face nuzzles against my hand and a soft smile forms on her sleeping face.You have no clue what you're doing doll.

I just sit there, unmoving. I was afraid to do anything and stop this, or wake her.I just wanted to enjoy this feeling.

She may be asleep but she's comforted by me. And even if she doesn't know it, that means the fucking world to me.Everything.

After a few hours, I begin to gently play with her hair with my other hand.So perfect for me.Curled up into my touch.Fucking perfect.

I spend the entire night here, unmoving, just savoring this feeling. Comforting her in any way I can by tracing her back or playing with her hair...

She still has my other hand in her soft hold, the silky skin of her cheek pressed against my palm.

I could stay here forever and be so fucking happy.But I know I can't.Because when she wakes up, she'll no longer be comforted by me. She'll be fucking terrified.

So when I see the sun begin to rise, it takes all the restraint I have to gently pull my hand out of her soft hold.A little frown forms on her sleeping face and it nearly kills me.I'm so sorry doll.

I press a soft kiss to her cheek, loving the way her skin feels against my lips. I look over her sleeping body once more before getting up, but I need to do something before I leave.I open her fucking curtains.

# Chapter 9- Hailey

I step out of my bathroom in some flimsy shorts and a little tank top. I don't ever drink tea but I needed an excuse to go downstairs, maybe I'd even catch him...I carefully walk down the steps, looking around. I see nothing. But I feel him. He's here.

I grin widely as I make my way over the kitchen. I know he's hiding somewhere close by. I can sense his eyes burning into my skin.

I hop up onto the countertop waiting for my water to heat up. I feel like a giddy teenager whose crush just said hi to her. Except in my case I had a large man watching me in my own home. Better in my opinion.

I grabbed my mug of tea and rushed back upstairs, literally giggling when I made it to my room. Okay, he's forgiven now.

After I sip my tea, I slip under a blanket and turn my lights off. But I'm much too excited to fall asleep. I close my eyes and curl up on my side. And I wait.

After a while, I hear the softest creek of my bedroom door opening. Aw, so considerate. He doesn't want to wake me...

I keep my breathing as slow and steady as I can as he approaches me. I can smell him. I'd recognize the scent anywhere.

After another few minutes, I feel my bed dip slightly. I've never been more awake in my fucking life and it takes everything in me to keep pretending to sleep.

I feel his hand brush the curls out away from my face, so gently. Gentleness I wouldn't expect him to have.

His fingers trace over the features of my face, then along the skin of my exposed arm and I fucking melt.

I can't help myself but want more. I hum softly, pretending to be asleep as I wrap my arm around his wrist, pulling it closer. I snuggle into it, loving the way his hand feels against my cheek. He's so warm. It almost lulls me to sleep before I can finish enjoying this.

I can't help but smile at the sensation, curling up into his touch. I can feel him still completely, not even hearing his breathing for a few moments. I caught him off guard. Hah

With him exactly where I want, I allow myself to finally drift off. His warmth, his scent, it's like a drug that completely relaxes my body and I find no resistance to falling asleep that night.

The last thing I remember is his fingers toying with my curls before I go into a deep sleep.

•••

When I wake up the next morning, he's gone. I pout slightly, but I expected him to. I know he doesn't want to scare me. It's cute

I stand up out of bed, stretching out my body from my blissful sleep last night. I look over at the bright sun flooding my room and I smile widely.The curtains. Open.

I laugh to myself at the sight, loving how he can't stand to have his eyes off me.I stand over by the window, giving a good show of me stretching out my body this morning.And I can feel it.His eyes.

I practically skip down the stairs to the kitchen as I make myself a pot of coffee. Taking my mug, I curl up in the loveseat by my window, reading a book while I sip on my latte.

I wonder what it would be like if he was here.Cuddled up against him in the morning, feeling his arms around me....Perfect.

I get up eventually, making myself a big brunch. Pancakes, eggs, bacon, fruit... all of it.It's a great morning.

I dance to some music as I cook and I know his eyes are trained on my hips.I sit on my kitchen counter and eat when I'm finished, my gaze drifting out to the window. I can't see him at the moment, but I know he's there.

After I'm finished, I hop off the counter, wanting to head to the gym before I work later tonight.I slip on some leggings and a sports bra before heading out to my car.

I hope he follows me today.I just want to see him.

Once I'm done with my warm up, I spot a large frame in the back of the gym, shielded by a big hoodie.Very inconspicuous baby.

I smile to myself as I begin my workout, starting with squats, giving him a good view of my ass.I can practically feel him burning holes into my skin with his eyes.He keeps glaring at any man who looks in my direction.Ad orable. I smile to myself.

I go throughout the rest of my workout, time moving by incredibly fast. My skin is glistening with sweat and a few curls are stuck to my damp face as I finish.

I take extra time stretching out today, wanting to give him something to think about later.I think I'm having too much fun with this...

I get up once I'm done, hopping into my car before driving back home.I had another idea...I grabbed some things before heading into the shower. I knew he'd be here soon.

I rinse off, covering my body in coconut scented body wash.Once I'm done, I do my hair up into a bun, taking a few curls out around my face.I've noticed he likes it when I wear my hair up.

When I step out of the bathroom, but I'm not wrapped in a towel like normal. I chose a little lacy black thong and a matching bra.Thought he'd like this... it's similar to the pair he stole.

I smirk when I feel his eyes on me immediately.I take my time massaging my coconut lotion into my skin, giving him a perfect view of my body.

After I've had my fun, I turn around and put on some black pants and a tank top for work.I put on a light amount of makeup tonight, just wanting to look good for him.

I wanted to make him sweat...

I head downstairs, grabbing myself a quick snack before heading off to work.This'll be fun.

# Chapter 10- Ryder

She is going to kill me with this shit. First earlier today when she stretched her pretty body out right in front of the window...

Then going out to the gym, God the way her ass looked in those leggings almost gave me a stroke. I had to stop myself from shooting every man in the building for being in her presence. I'm loosing my mind here.

And now... when she stepped out of that fucking bathroom. My jaw dropped. She was a fucking goddess.

Only in a tiny black thong and a bra that pushed her tits together perfectly. They had a soft lace trim on them, fitting her body so damn nice. Who are you wearing this shit for doll? Hm?

I couldn't even bring myself to worry about that at the moment with how fucking hard my cock is at the sight of her. She has her hair up in a bun with a few strands falling along her face. Fucking perfect.

I watch greedily as she massages her lotion all over her body, almost in fucking slow motion. Like she's my own personal fucking fantasy. She is.

What I wouldn't give to have my hands all over her, eating her sweet pussy out till she cums on my face. Fuck. Fuck. Fuck.

My jaw clenches as she turns around, bending over to grab some clothes for work. Giving me a perfect view of her ass in that little thong. God damn.

I stare as she slides on a pair of black pants and a tight black tank top. She even puts on a bit of makeup today. Not that she fucking needs any.

She strolls out of the house minutes later, a big smile on her face.I wonder what has her smiling so much lately...I want to be the one that makes her smile.Me.

I get into my car a few moments after she leaves for work, driving myself over to the bar. The view of her in that black set just keeps replaying in my mind like a fucking movie. I can't stop it if I wanted to.

I've been waiting in my car outside her work for 45 minutes begging my dick to calm the fuck down.

When I finally collect myself, I make my way inside. Her eyes move up to me for a moment, and I swear there's a smirk on her face when she sees me. This little fucking temptress.

There's already a few people at the bar and I go take a seat on one of the barstools.I patiently wait, watching as she makes a few drinks before making her way over to me with a smile.

"Hey there" she grins at me "Jack and Coke?" She asks, and I smirk widely.She remembers"That sounds perfect doll" i reply smoothly.

I remembered she liked that the other night...I can see the soft blush on her cheeks before she turns away, and my smile widens.My girl is so responsive... I love it.

She hands me my drink moments later and I thank her before she goes back to work.I watch with admiration as she glides around the bar easily, handling any rowdy guests.

It pisses me off anytime someone makes a flirty comment with her or tries to get her number, but she always declines.Cause she's such a good girl for me.The crowd begins to slow down as I sit there just taking her in.She looks up at me before walking over with a smile.

"You're here nearly every night for hours, and you only order one drink... how come?" She asks me with a smirk.

"You trying to get me drunk doll?" I reply, smirking as her eyes narrow playfully.Feisty. I love it. "No- I wasn't... just wondering what keeps you here all night" she says with a grin.

I lean closer, resting my arms against the bar-top as my smirk grows"Hm, I don't know. Maybe it's just the ambiance."

Her eyes flicker down at my arms for a moment before looking back up at me"The ambiance huh?" She laughs softly

I just smile up at her "Yeah. The ambiance."I extend my hand out to her."I'm Ryder."

She raises a brow at me for a moment, smiling before shaking my hand. God her hand feels so soft.

She doesn't say anything, just stares there at me for a few moments"And your name is?" I add, internally smirking.I know your name doll.

She looks at me for a moment, grinning."Hailey" she responds.I nod, letting go of her soft hand."Nice to meet you Hailey" I grin

"You too Ryder" Fuck. My name sounds so fucking good from her lips.I've never liked my name so much until this moment, because here it sounds fucking perfect.

She smirks for a moment, almost as if she can tell my brain is short-circuiting before walking away.She knows my name..My girl knows my name.I feel like I'm fucking 12 years old with a crush.Fucking love sick idiot.Just for you doll.

I spend the last hour or so watching her as she makes drinks, talking to a few other regulars.I keep getting flashbacks from earlier that reminded me exactly what is underneath her clothes.

Once she begins cleaning up, I place a fifty on the bar for her, getting out of my seat.She looks up at me with those pretty fucking eyes."Ryder? Would you walk me to my car? Please?" She asks me so sweetly.

Anything you fucking want angel.Was going to walk you anyways."Of course, I'll wait for you" I smile at her.

She runs off to grab her things before coming back out to me, I hold the door open for her as we leave the bar.

I walk out with her to her car, the cool air causing her to shiver in her tank top.Trying to be a gentleman for once, I take off my jacket, putting it around her shoulders."Thank you" she smiles sweetly at me.I nodShe looks so fucking good in my clothes.

When we reach her car, she moves to give me my jacket back."Keep it" I tell her firmlyShe nods softly with a soft smile as she gets into her car."Night Ryder" she tells me

"Goodnight doll"

# Chapter 11- Hailey

------

I smiled as he walked in, coming straight to the bar. Feeling bold today huh?

I make my way over to him, asking him if he'd like his usual order "That sounds perfect doll" he replies. Fuck, I love when he calls me that.

I turn away before he can see my reaction, making his drink. Once I hand it to him, I have to go back to the other customers, distracting myself by working.

I can feel his eyes on me the whole time though. They never leave me. I catch a few glances at him as I work, just casually sipping on his drink, watching my every move.

As the bar slows down a little more, I decide to push him a little more. I was feeling bored.

"You're here nearly every night for hours, and you only order one drink... how come?" I ask him. I know exactly why you're here. He doesn't even bat an eye at the question, answering me confidently as he tells me "I don't know, maybe it's the ambiance" The smirk he puts on gives me goosebumps.

Yeah right it's the fucking ambiance of this shitty bar that keeps you coming back. I fight to keep from laughing in his face.

When I question his answer, he leans forward, his arms set against the counter between us. Those fucking arms could crush someone. Or throw me over his fucking shoulder before he fucks the shit out of me...

His voice stops my train of thought "I'm Ryder" he tells me, extending his hand. Ryder... it suits him. I take his hand, shaking it slowly. We just look at each other for a few moments before he looks as me with a smirk. "And your name is?"

I have to hold my breath for a moment so that I don't laugh. You know my name. "Hailey""Nice to meet you Hailey"

I grin."You too Ryder" I smirk as I emphasize his name, watching his eyes glaze over, fucking speechless. It's too easy.

I walk off with a smirk, making some last few drinks for the night before cleaning up. I see Ryder get up to leave, and I speak up before he can go."Ryder? Could you walk me to my car? Please?" I ask in my sweetest voice.

I can see the proud smile come over his face as he tells me he'll wait for me. I laugh softly as I grab my things. Stroking his fucking ego. Men are so simple.

I come back out to meet him and he holds the door for me. Adorable how he acts like such a gentleman. I know you Ryder. As we walk out to my car, the night air causes me to shiver, and like the adorable idiot he is, He puts his jacket on me.

Once I'm at my car, I offer it back to him, but am glad when he tells me to keep it. Didn't want to give it back. I smile as I drive off, knowing he'll come to see me again tonight.

I head up to my room when I get home, wanting to get comfortable. I slip on a lace thong, the kind that he likes, and throw an oversized t shirt over me.

Then I head back downstairs to the kitchen, craving some cookies. I get out all of the ingredients, humming softly as I add them together into a large bowl.

I mix everything together, forming the dough into balls as the oven heats up. Once everything is ready, I place them in the oven to bake.

I can't help but lick the spoon I used to mix the dough. The extra raw cookie dough is the best part. That, and I can feel his eyes on me.

I clean up the kitchen while the cookies bake, the sweet smell filling the house. Once they're finished baking, I take them out of the oven, moving over to the couch.

Sitting back, I finish an episode of my favorite show as I munch on a few cookies. It was a late night so I don't last long before getting tired.

I leave the rest of the cookies out, wondering if he would like them. Look at me, such a good hostess. I smile

I make my way up to my bedroom, curling up underneath a plush blanket. Once I turn my lights out, all I have to do is wait.

Not even a few minutes later, I hear the faint sound of my back door being closed. A smile forms on my face.

I close my eyes and slow my breathing, pretending to be asleep. Waiting patiently, I hear him walk into my room softly. He stops in front of me and I can hear him curse. His fingers gently drag along my exposed thigh, sending shivers down my body.

My shirt has ridden up and he can tell I'm not wearing any shorts. Perfect.

Now I just wanted him closer. But he was hesitant after last night, I could tell. I needed to think of how I could get him to touch me.

I started to shift slightly in my fake sleep, making him back away. I furrowed my eyebrows together as I let out a soft whimper, as if I was having a bad dream. Come comfort me

Soon enough his thumb was rubbing along my cheek in a soothing manner, his other hand on my waist softly as he mumbles "Shh pretty girl, you're safe" I let my actions settle, as if I'm relaxing back into sleep as I lean into his touch. Too easy.

He presses a few kisses against my shoulder and my cheek, causing me to smile softly. "So perfect" he whispers

I curl up closer into his touch, humming in contentment. This is what I need. Him. Here. Keeping me safe. I feel him lie back next to me, letting me sink into him further.

I rest my head against his arm as his fingers trace up and down my back softly. The feeling puts me into the best sleep of my life.

# Chapter 12- Ryder

When I get to her house, she's downstairs in the kitchen, making some cookie dough. After she puts them in the oven, she brings the spoon she used to her mouth, licking off the excess dough slowly. She closes her eyes like she's savoring it.

She looks so good I feel like I'm dreaming.

She soon settles in on the couch, eating a few of the cookies while she watches some tv. She has some chocolate on the edge of her lips and all I want is to taste it. Or taste her.

I can tell she's getting tired as she gets up, moving up to her bedroom. When the lights turn off, it's my time to come in.

The second I enter the door, the smell of those delicious cookies hits me. I'd kill for a taste. Like the devil is tempting me, I see a plate out on her kitchen counter full of the extra cookies. She wouldn't notice... would she? I come closer, they look so good.

I just needed a taste. She'd never know.

I grab one of the cookies on top, taking a bite. I hum softly at the sweetness, they're fucking perfect. Just the thought that she was the one who made them, used her hands...Makes them so much better.I quickly finish the cookie, making my way upstairs to see my girl.

I open her door to see her peacefully sleeping, the blanket only covering part of her perfect body."Fuck" I mumbleShe's not wearing any shorts.I can tell as her shirt has risen up in her sleep, exposing the smooth curve of her hip to me.I have to feel her.

My fingers graze up the length of her thigh, dragging along the fabric of her t shirt that just barely covers her. My own personal angel.

After a few minutes, I remove my hand, not wanting to risk anything after last night.It was so damn hard for me to pull away from her. All curled up into my touch....

Her body shifts a bit, breaking me out of my train of thought. I back away at first, worrying she's waking up.

Then her face contorts into a scared expression, frowning as she lets out a whine.Oh my poor girl is having a nightmare...I can't stand to let her be like this

I quickly come over to her, rubbing my thumb back and forth over her cheek as my other hand holds her waist securely.

"Shh pretty girl, you're safe" I whisper softly.Her body relaxes more and leans into my touch.Fucking adorable.I press a few light kisses against her soft skin, first her shoulder, then leading up to her cheek.She smiles softly."So perfect" I mumble in aweShe's drawn to me. Even in her sleep.

My logical reasoning goes out the window as I sit back on her bed, lying next to her.This is so fucking stupid of me.But it's all worth it when she leans closer into my body, her head nestled against my arm.My perfect angel.I trace her back up and down softly, coaxing her into a deep sleep as the night goes on.

I can still see the chocolate on her lips from earlier, and I can't help myself. I gently wipe it off with my thumb, feeling the soft skin of her lips that makes me smile.

I bring my thumb to my lips, slowly sucking the sweet chocolate off. Savoring it. Tasting it for as long as I can. Perfect.

I lie there with her for hours, not moving a fucking inch. There's a part of me that wants to just grab her and pull her on top of me, wrapping her body around me as I hold her as close as possible...But I don't. I have to be patient. My girl deserves that. So I'll wait for her. But that doesn't mean I can't enjoy this now.

I let my hands travel through her smooth hair, over her pretty throat, down her soft arm, along her creamy thighs.... Everywhere. I could admire her for the rest of my life. She's the most precious thing I've ever seen.

•••

I've been shot before and I swear the pain of pulling away from her in the morning is so much worse. I'd take a bullet any day to keep her in my arms. But I have to let go.

I hold the back of her head gently and I replace my arm with her pillow. I fucking hate this. I look back sadly as the bright sunlight fills her room, her skin glowing. I'll see you soon doll.

I quietly leave her house, making sure to lock the door behind me. I make my way back to my car, needing to head back to my apartment for a little while. I hadn't been there since I came back into town, too worried about seeing my girl.

But I was in desperate need of a shower and had some paperwork I needed to follow up on. I'd see her tonight when she came into work.

I stepped into the bar later that night wearing some black jeans and a tight black t shirt that showed my arms.I had a hunch she liked them...Her eyes flicker up to mine, a slight smile forming on her face as she sees me.Hey pretty girl.

I settle down at the bar, watching her rushing to take orders.She looked so good tonight.She had her hair clipped back behind her head, just some mascara on her pretty lashes.

She wore this tight bodysuit and some black jeans that hugged tightly around her hips.Good enough to eat.

Eventually, she makes her way over to me with a smile."Jack and Coke?" She asks me"You know me so well doll" I smirkShe rolls her eyes at me, grinning as she walks away.I know you love it doll, don't even try me.

Minutes later she comes back with my drink in hand, quickly running off to go take someone else's order.I sip on my drink, enjoying my view when I notice someone knock their drink over the bar, the glass shattering.My girl quickly goes over to pick up the shards.

Asshole doesn't even fucking apologize.Fucker.

As she picks up the pieces, I hear her hiss softly, seeing she cut herself.She sighs, throwing out the shards of glass before getting up, blood dripping down her hand.I'm in front of her before I even realize it."Here, let me see" I say softly.

"It's just a little cut, I'm-" she starts "Let me see." I say firmer.She gulps softly, giving me her hand.I grab a first aid kit in the corner, wiping off her hand before gently cleaning the cut.I disinfect it before putting a clean bandage over top."There." I say softly, smiling down at her blushing face.Do I make you nervous doll?

# Chapter 13- Hailey

------

I grin as I come down to the kitchen the next day, seeing he ate one of the cookies.I knew he wouldn't be able to resist...I go clean up around my place a bit before getting ready for work, wearing something I think he'd like.

•••

I smile when I see him walk in, sitting at the bar.I grab him his drink as usual, working to make some other orders until some dude knocked his glass over.I watch as it lands a few feet away from me, shattering behind the bar. Great.

I sigh, going to pick it up, accidentally cutting my palm while doing so.Fuck this.When I get back up, my eyes widen. Ryder is standing right in front of me, so close my breathing stops for a moment.Hey there stalker.

He insists I give him my hand and I finally give in. He seems like someone not to debate this with.

His touch is so gentle as he cleans the cut, and I'm distracted by his bulging arms flexing slightly the entire time.Yum.I've never seen him in short sleeves before, and let's just say the jackets he normally wears were not doing him justice.Damn.

When he's done, I snap out of my trance, looking back up at him.I mumble a small thank you before going back to work.He just returns to his seat, casually sipping on his drink like nothing happened.His eyes on me like always.

After a few hours, he tilts his head at me to come back over to him.I walk over with a smile.

"Could you make me your favorite drink?" He asks me.Hm, this is new..."2 drinks tonight Ryder? Feeling wild are we?" I reply with a smile.

"Only for you doll" he says and the biggest fucking smile comes on my face. I can't even stop it.

"Alright then" I laugh, walking off to make him something I'd like.I make up a raspberry martini, laughing to myself at the thought of this huge man drinking a cute fruity cocktail.Oh I'm absolutely enjoying this too much.

"Here you go sir" I grin, handing him the drink.His eyes get darker for a second when I call him that.Interesting... good to know.He grins at me as he takes a sip. "Not your usual kinda drink huh?" I tease

"No... but it's surprisingly good" he grins at me.

I smile back at him before going back to working.I notice him finish the drink later that night.He actually liked it.

Ryder stays till I close like usual, waiting for me at the door. He doesn't even ask me this time as he holds the door for me, walking me out to my car.I'm wearing the jacket he gave me the other night and he grins at the fact."The jacket. It looks good on you" he tells me

I grin, "well now you're not getting it back""Good." He replies

We get to my car and he opens the door for me as I get in."Goodnight Ryder" I smile up at him"Goodnight pretty girl" Fucking stop it.He's getting too good at making me blush.

I can see him still smiling in my mirror as I drive off.He's loving this.

•••

I make my way home for the night, heading upstairs to my room.Stepping into the bathroom, I take off my clothes before getting into the shower.

I let the warm water run over me, rubbing coconut body wash all over my body.

I spend more time than usual on my skincare once I'm out of the shower, putting my hair in a bun.He thinks he's the only one who knows how to tease?Coming tonight and flexing his muscles and taking care of me and shit.I'll show him teasing...

I step out into my bedroom, just in a silky black robe that comes down to my thighs.I take my coconut lotion, massaging it into my skin as I feel his gaze all over me.But I'm nowhere near finished.

I then lie back on my bed, trailing my hands along my exposed cleavage, then down over my thighs.I can feel my body heating up from his staring .Perfect.I spread my thighs open, knowing he can't completely see me, but he'll be able to see enough...

I trail my fingers down the inside of my thighs, making my way towards my pussy.I was going to torture him with this...I slowly began to touch myself, my fingers gliding through my wetness.

As I continued, I felt the loss of his gaze for a few minutes...Maybe it was too much for him...But then I feel it again.Hotter.Closer.He came inside...

Out of the corner of my eye, I can see my bedroom door cracked open, and I can feel him watching. But I don't care. If anything, it turned me on more.

My fingers moved faster as soft moans left my lips. This felt fucking incredible, I could feel how badly he wanted me. And it was addictive.

I worked my fingers inside me, my moans getting louder as I get closer to my orgasm. My heart is racing, the feeling of him there only making this so much more sinful. It felt way too good to stop.

My orgasm rushed over me as I moaned, wanting him to hear me. My breathing was ragged as I came down from my high, still feeling his eyes burning into me. So fucking good.

I fought the urge to look over at my bedroom door, I didn't want to scare him off…So I just simply laid back in bed, turning off my lights as I pulled a blanket over me. I closed my eyes, lying there for what felt like hours.

My heart was racing. I was waiting. Waiting to see what he'd do. I heard my bedroom door creak open softly…

# Chapter 14- Ryder

I'm having too much fun seeing her all flustered. I just want to hear her sweet voice again. So I ask her to make me her favorite drink.

I know, basic move, but her smile tells me she enjoys it.

She comes back with this red, fruity cocktail and hands it to me, laughing when I take a sip. Little does she know I'd drink anything she made with a smile. I don't care as long as her hands made it.

She keeps glancing back at me as she works, making me grin. If I didn't know better, I'd say you're checking me out doll...

At the end of the night, I walk her out to her car as usual, admiring her in my jacket. I can't believe she's wearing it again.

"Goodnight Ryder" "Goodnight pretty girl" I can't miss the way her cheeks heat up at my words. I fucking love when she blushes. My favorite thing.

She drives off and I soon follow behind her, eager to have my eyes on her again. When I arrive, her bedroom light is on, but she's not there.

In the shower I'm guessing.

After a while, she appears again in this little silky black robe. Fuck, that's a new look.

I could get used to this.

The soft fabric reaches the tops of her thighs, and her cleavage just pokes through the v.Stunning.

She starts to lather her body in lotion and I'm practically drooling.Once she's finished, she lies back in her bed with a mischievous smile on her face.What's my girl up to?

I watch attentively as her fingers trace around her cleavage, grazing over her stomach before going over her thighs.Oh fuck.

Her hands start skimming over her inner thighs as they part open, and I practically trip over myself trying to get a better view.My pretty little vixen...

When her hand disappears between her thighs, I loose all my composure, rushing around to her back door.I need to be there.Hear her.

I slip inside, quickly making my way upstairs, thanking whatever god is out there that there is a crack open in her bedroom door.I can fucking hear her little whines and moans from here.And fuck if they aren't the best things I've ever heard.

My dick is straining against my jeans as I make it to her doorway, watching her hand work between her pretty thighs.The sexiest thing I've ever seen.

Her lips are parted in pleasure as moans slip out of her mouth, echoing in my mind.She's trying to kill me.I can't even fucking breathe.

I stifle down a groan as her fingers slip inside her wet pussy, her back arching up at the feeling.Her head falls back, her eyes falling closed.I can tell she's close.

Her moans sound so fucking desperate.I have to grip onto her fucking doorframe to keep myself from diving between those thighs of hers.I'm losing my sanity.

I watch as she cums, committing every fucking detail to memory. Not even blinking.The sounds. The way she looks.Her fucking thighs trembling in pleasure.It's too fucking much.I'd kill anyone else who sees her like this.This is only for me.

When she calms down from her orgasm, she just curls up in bed casually, turning off the lights.I watch as her eyes shut, and she pulls a blanket over her silk covered body.I'm literally frozen.I honestly am not sure if I died and went to fucking heaven.This feels a whole lot like my heaven.

After a long while, I finally move into her room, approaching her sleeping figure.

My fingers move to rake through her messy curls, adoring the way they feel against my fingers.I'd like to pull them while I fuck her pretty pussy from behind-I let out a deep sigh.

I look down at her hand…The same hand that she used to make herself cum so beautifully.I just need a little taste.This is bad. Risky.

I gently take her hand in mine, kneeling down.I bring my mouth to her hands.Then I oh so gently put her fingers into my mouth, softly sucking the release off of them.Fuck.So fucking good.I want to drown in it. My dick twitches painfully.

I slowly release her fingers, letting them fall back down.She's still asleep.I let out a breath of relief."So fucking good for me"

I sit down by her carefully, tracing over her pretty face. So beautiful.I place a light kiss on her cheek… then her neck… her collarbone… her arm…I lean down a press a few to her exposed thigh...And finally, I take her hand and place a kiss over her bandaged cut.My poor girl. So fucking lovely.

I lie back a bit, my back resting on her headboard as my legs stretch out next to her.I start playing with her pretty hair, admiring each ringlet.She moves slightly in her sleep, turning to rest her head on my thigh, one of her hands wrapping around my leg.My perfect fucking angel.Made for me and she doesn't even know it.

I smile down at her, relishing in her touch as I continue to play with her soft curls.I spend the rest of the night just watching her peaceful face.She looks so god damn innocent when she sleeps.But I know better doll.I've seen what you do when you think no one's watching...

I loose track of time, so fucking at peace with my beautiful girl sleeping on my lap.

I just trace over her soft skin until the sun comes up, forcing me to leave her.This is the worst part of my fucking day.I slowly guide her off my body, replacing me with a pillow.I wish I could stay with you sweetheart.

I press a kiss to her jaw before getting up, taking one last look at my sleeping girl before leaving.You'll be all mine soon doll.And then you'll wake up in my arms every day.

# Chapter 15- Hailey

-------------------------------------------------

I hold my breath when I feel his mouth around my fingers. Tasting me. I can't even function. I hope he can't hear how fucking hard my heart is pounding right now.

"So fucking good for me" he mumbles You have no idea.

I feel his lips press all over my exposed skin, softly, like he's savoring every inch. Then finally he presses a kiss over my cut, like he's kissing it better. He can't be doing this to me.

I then feel his fingers go to play with my hair, the sensation sending relaxing tingles down my body. The bed dips slightly as he sits next to me, a smile forming on my face.

I slowly move to curl up into him, my head resting on his thigh while my arm curls around his leg. Silently pleading him to stay. Part of me just wants to tell him I know...But then he'll think I'm insane. Maybe he wouldn't want me anymore.

So I just enjoy the moment while I can, drifting off into a blissful sleep.

•••

He's gone the next morning as I wake up to my cold bed. Still smells like him.As I move downstairs to the kitchen, I stop for a moment.He's still here.I can feel his energy in the room. His eyes.Clingy today hm?

I go through my day as I normally do, trying not to show any signs of suspicion.But I can't help every now and then but to look around the room, wondering if I'll see him there, watching.I never do.

But I can tell his need is growing... he's becoming riskier... more invasive...I like it.

I get ready for work, taking my time walking around the house in hopes of catching a glance... a shadow...

I eventually give up, heading out to my car.

•••

He comes in later than usual that night while I'm working, but I don't question it.It's a Saturday night so the bar is packed.

I'm busy making drinks when he sits down at the bar, just watching me.I finally make my way over to him, apologizing for taking so long."Don't apologize to me love" he tells me, grinning.I just shake my head, smiling back

"A Jack and Coke then?"

"I'll take whatever that raspberry drink you made me last night was... pretty good doll" he says, surprising me.He actually liked it.

"Okay then" I grin, walking offI come back with his drink and the rest of the night goes as usual.

Once I'm done, Ryder waits for me at the door and we head out to my car.I reach for my car door, but before I can, he stops me, lightly grabbing my arm."Hold on- you have a flat" he says, pointing down at my tire that's sunken into the ground.

He kneels down to look at it, pointing out a shiny silver nail"Looks like you ran over a nail there" he saysOh did I?"Oh wow, I didn't even notice" I say, looking down at his stupid grin.

"Want some help changing it doll?" He asksWow, my hero I think, internally rolling my eyes.

"Yeah, I have no idea how to change a tire" I laugh softly.I do.

But I just love how adorable he looks right now feeling like my night and shining armor.So I'll let him change my tire.Pretty sure he stuck the nail in it anyways.

I definitely don't regret my decision as I sit back, biting my bottom lip as he jacks up my car.His muscles are flexing so hard they look like they'll rip right through his shirt.Who needs a shirt anyways?

He sets the spare tire in place, tightening the lug nuts in place so the tire is secure.My own personal sexy mechanic.I kinda dig it.

"There we go, all set" he says, wiping the sweat off his forehead.

"Thank you- you're a life saver" I tell him sweetly

"No problem doll" he grins so wide.Aw look at him, so proud of himself.

I tell him goodnight, hopping in my car before driving home.God I wish he would just fucking ask me out.He's already tasted me... the least he could do is take a girl out to dinner.

But I guess he isn't really someone who takes a normal approach to dating... as in not stalking them...

When I got home, I went upstairs to rinse off and get out of my work clothes. It's nearly 3 am and all I want to do is go to sleep, and have my hot stalker come in and hold me. I'm so easy to please truly.

I put on a tank top and some underwear, slipping under my blankets. Lights out. Come and find me baby.

After about 20 minutes, I hear him slip into my bedroom. Keep a straight face Hailey. He presses a kiss onto my shoulder and I hope it's dark enough that he can't see my blush. He lays beside me, moving me gently to lie down on his chest. Loving this. I bend one of my thighs up so that it's sprawled across his lap, showing my exposed skin. He groans in appreciation.

I smile softly against his chest as I feel his fingers trailing down my spine, relaxing me. His other hand moves to my thigh, rubbing it up and down for a while. I can feel the roughness of his hand against my soft skin… perfect

His hand moves higher, cupping my ass as he lets out a low hum. I think I just felt his dick twitch against my thigh.

That did not feel small.

He softly massages my the flesh, seeming to really be enjoying himself. I'm really trying not to laugh here. It feels good though.

His scent and his soothing touch puts me to sleep before I'd want to, forcing me to drift off in his arms. Just how I imagined…

# Chapter 16- Ryder

I put my hood up, making sure to turn away from the cameras that surround the bar. I take the sharp nail from my pocket, puncturing her tire. It's harmless really. I just want more time with her.

I make sure it's a large enough hole so that air leaks out over her shift before finally heading inside. To see my pretty girl.

The night goes on watching her, and I surprise her by asking for that fruity drink she made me the other night. I just wanted to see her smile.

...

I wait eagerly by the door for her at the end of the night, walking her back to her car. I grab her arm gently before she hops in, "Hold on- looks like you have a flat" I tell her.

She looks down at where I pointed, smiling for a moment before her expression turns to surprise. "Oh wow, I didn't even notice" she tells me

Oh my pretty girl, what would you do without me?

I offer to help her fix it, hoping she says yes.I just wanted to be near her a bit longer...I smile widely when she admits she has no idea how to change a tire.Don't worry doll, I'll fix it.

My grin widens when I get the chance to help her... I just love being able to take care of my girl.Even if I did cause the problem.

I kneel down, jacking up her car before taking my time removing the tire.I can feel her eyes on me the whole time.Look at me all you want doll.I'm all yours.

I replace the tire with the spare, tightening it in place for her.She beams up at me when I'm finished, thanking me in her sweet voice.God I love that sound.

I watch her drive off with a smile, knowing I'd have her in my arms soon.

•••

Later that night, I slip inside her room, approaching her bed.I press a kiss against the smooth skin of her shoulder before lying back next to her.I just wanted to hold her. So bad.I ever so carefully drag her closer to me, praying she doesn't wake up.

Her head rests against my chest and she curls up into me like a fucking cat.That's right doll, my perfect girl.

One of her legs slips out from under the blanket, draping over my lap. I can see now that she's only wearing these little lace panties.Fuck.I can't help but let out a soft groan at how good she looks.The smooth skin of her thighs so fucking inviting.

One of my hands traces soft shapes over her back to keep her relaxed.The other travels to her thigh that's so perfectly displayed for me.Begging for me to touch.Such a good girl. Even in her sleep.

Her skin feels like silk as I trail my hand up and down her thigh. I can't help but go higher, feeling over her perfect fucking ass, cupping it in my hand.Fucking perfect, I humI gently massage over the soft flesh, my dick jumping at how perfect it feels in my hand.

I just stay right here for hours.Nothing has ever felt as perfect as having her sleeping in my arms.I want this for rest of my god damn life.

I take her hand, threading our fingers together as she sleeps so soundly against my chest.

•••

I don't pull away from her until later in the morning, when I see her begin to stir.I softly roll her off of me, my chest aching as I step out of her room just as she wakes up.

I started to stick around in her house during the day...I was already being too risky so fuck it.

She came downstairs eventually, still wearing those panties and that flimsy tank top.She just strolls around the kitchen with a grin, her skin practically glowing in the morning sun.What a fucking sight.

Stopping, she hops up on the kitchen counter, sitting her pretty ass on the granite as she waits for her coffee to brew.I've never been jealous of a counter before.

I watch as she sips her coffee, mixing a bunch of ingredients together in a large bowl.Looks like she's making some sort of baked good.

She pours the batter into a muffin pan, setting it in the oven to bake.I bite my lip as she walks into her living room, seeing the curve of her ass with each step.Damn.She smiles softly, sitting down with a book by the window while she waits.

She looks so fucking edible.Her eyes drift across the pages smoothly, her body slowly relaxing.

About 40 minutes later, she pops back up to take the muffins out.They look fucking delicious.She picked out one, taking a big bite.And moans.

She has to be fucking with me honestly.This incredible fucking woman is torturing me, and she doesn't even know it.

She soon goes back upstairs to change before heading to the gym. She steps out wearing a dark green set today that brings out her eyes.Those pretty fucking eyes.

As she leaves, I decided to take the time to explore her house more. Learn everything I could about her.What she likes...I wanted to give her everything.

I went through her kitchen, taking notes of all her favorite snacks, fruits, ice cream.Anything.I've noticed she likes to bake too.How fucking adorable.

I went to her closet, looking over her clothes. She'd look good in fucking anything, but I wanting to know what she liked, the sizes, colors...For when I can buy her everything she wants.

Then, the bathroom, searching through all the different products for her hair and skin.I wanted to learn all of it.So I could do it for her when she was tired.

Once I was finished, I slipped out of her place before she got back, knowing I needed to go home and get changed before seeing her tonight.I wanted to look good for my girl of course.

I took a shower, putting on some jeans and one of those t shirts she seems to like on me.I spray on some cologne, shaving the stubble on my face before heading to her work.Time to go see my pretty girl.

# Chapter 17- Hailey

I went down to the kitchen this morning, grinning when I felt his eyes on me immediately. Never would have thought I'd be so into this shit.

I sit up on the kitchen counter so he can see me as I wait for my coffee to brew. I think he likes the view...He definitely enjoyed himself last night.

I can't believe I've lasted this long without accidentally reacting or making a sound while I'm so called "sleeping".

I decided to make up some muffins since I was craving something sweet. Mixing up the batter, I put some chocolate chips in it before baking.

I sit back, curling up in my seat while I wait for them to bake. I pull out a book to read, but honestly I don't even process a single word. All I can think about is how close he is right now... somewhere nearby but just out of my sight. When I hear my timer go off, I pop up, getting the muffins from the oven.

After a few minutes, I take a bite of one, letting out a soft moan on purpose like I'm enjoying them just that much. They're good, but not that good. Just wanted to tease him a bit...

After I'm done, I head back upstairs, getting ready to go to the gym.

He doesn't follow me there today, but I decided to just focus on my workout. I'm sure I'd see him later.

I make it back home afterwards, noticing he's not there either. Strange.

I'm walking upstairs to my bathroom to take a shower, and notice some of my products aren't where I left them. Snooping around huh? Rolling my eyes, I finally step under the hot water, letting it relax my thoughts.

Once I'm finished, I pull my curls back into a low bun before putting on some clothes for work tonight. I make myself a sandwich, quickly eating before getting on my way.

•••

Not long after my shift begins, I see his large frame walk through the door, sitting down at the end of the bar. Looking over, I flash him a quick smile, letting him know I'll be over soon. I finish making some drinks, and before I can go over to him, a voice stops me.

"Hey sweetheart" I stop in my tracks, turning around. No.

I look up to see my ex boyfriend wearing a confident grin as he greets me as if we're old friends. We're not. "Sam." I say back coldly. "I'm at work. Busy."

"Oh come on... don't be like that honey." he says, leaning forward. Why can't I move. Fucking pathetic.

"I don't have time to talk right now Sam..." I get out softly. He reaches forward, grabbing my face. His fingers sink harshly into my jaw. Anyone watching would see his friendly smile, but his eyes tell me not to fuck around. Taunting me. "What? You don't have time for me anymore-"

He's cut off by Ryder pulling him back roughly. Thank fuck. I rub my jaw softly, silent. Embarrassed.

"I think she said to leave her alone." Ryder says in a terrifyingly calm voice. He's absolutely glaring at Sam like he's the fucking scum of the earth. He pretty much is.

"Who are you? A new fucking bouncer or something?" Sam spits at him, trying to shake Ryders hand from him.

"Nah. Just someone who's more than happy to pound your fucking face in if you make her frown" Ryder replies, tightening his grip on my ex. Fuck that's hot.

"You know this guy Hays?" Sam asks me, and I outwardly cringe at the nickname. Fucking hated when he called me that.

"You should leave Sam" I say softly. He frowns.

"I'll show you the way out" Ryder grins, practically dragging him out the door. I grin at the sight.

He doesn't do anything... just watches as Sam drives away before coming back inside. I make my way over to him. "Thank you... you didn't have to do that" I tell him, suddenly a bit nervous speaking to him. Embarrassed he saw me like that. Weak.

"Don't mention it" he says, looking at me with nothing but admiration. "Why don't you just make me one of those raspberry martinis you like, hm?" He says, sensing my nerves.

I nod, letting out a deep breath before I go make the drink, allowing myself to calm down. I set the drink in front of him, and he thanks me before I run off to take some more orders.

I felt on edge the rest of the night, but having his eyes on me gave me a sense of comfort. I knew he wouldn't let anything happen to me while he was there. By the end of the night, he waited at the door for me.

He put his hand lightly on my lower back, guiding me as he walked me out to my car.

Before I could get in, he stopped me, turning me around. "Give me your phone yeah?" He asks calmly

Confused, I handed it to him. He types something in on it before handing it back to me, showing me his contact in my phone. He gave me his number

"You call me if he bothers you ever again, alright?" He looks down at me, raising a brow. He's so close right now.

"It's really nothing I-" he cuts me off

"You'll call me." He says firmer "okay?" He asks, his fingers gently skimming over where Sam had gripped my jaw with a frown.

"Okay" I say softly, looking up at him. He's so fucking close to me.

We just stand there for a moment and I'm having trouble remembering how to breathe as he leans closer, gently tilting my head up so that my eyes stay on him.

"Good girl" he smiles softly.

I'm literally going to fall to the ground in a puddle.

He leans down, inches away from my lips. Oh my god. He closes the gap slowly, pressing a kiss to my lips, long and slow...

I let out an involuntary whimper when he pulls away. His lips feel so nice.

I can't say anything as he opens my car door. I just fall back into the seat in shock, not even processing as I drive off. He kissed me.

# Chapter 18- Ryder

The second that idiot goes and talks to my girl my fists clench.I don't fucking like him.Sweetheart? Really?She looks uncomfortable.

I'm already standing as he tells her"Don't be like that honey" Fucking prick.Who is this guy?And what the fuck does he have to do with my girl?

"I don't have time to talk right now Sam..." she says softly.I'm dealing with him the second he fucking does anything.

I watch as he reaches out to grab her and I see red.Before I know it I'm grabbing him, pulling him back."I think she said to leave her alone." I tell him with a calm kind of threat in my voice.

Try me. I dare you.

"Who are you? A fucking bouncer or something?" The guy spits out, looking pissed. Good.He tries to squirm out of my grip so I just grip him harder, smirking internally when he winces.Not a fucking chance.

"Nah. Just someone who's more than happy to pound your fucking face in if you make her frown" I say, meaning every last word.Nobody touches my girl.

"You know this guy Hays?" He asks, turning to look at my girl.Hays? God I want to kill him right here.

"You should leave Sam." She tells himGood fucking girl."I'll show you out" I tell him all too happily, taking the opportunity to drag him out the door.I watch as he drives off, making sure to take down his plate numbers.Stupid fucker.

I come back inside seeing my pretty girl all shaken up. Should've grabbed him the second he came in here. Before he had a chance to even speak to her.

She thanks me for taking care of him, looking nervous.Always doll. Always.I try and take her mind off things, ordering one of those drinks she likes from her.I just stay there quietly through the whole night, sensing she didn't want to talk about it.

When it came time for me to walk her out to her car, I tried to make her feel as safe and comfortable as possible.This guy was still bugging me though.

Before she could get in her car, I stopped her, gently turning her to face me.I asked her for her phone and she handed it over, looking up at me confused.I typed my number in her contacts, handing it back.

"You call me if he bothers you ever again, yeah?" I tell her softly, trying not to scare her.I just wanted to make sure she's safe.She tries to tell me not to worry, that it's not a big deal but I cut her off.

You are the most fucking important thing in my world. It is a big deal.

"You call me. Okay?" I say firmer."Okay" she replies softly, just looking up at me.Fuck she looks so damn pretty.Keep your eyes on me doll.

"Good girl" I tell her and I can practically see her eyes dilate.Fucking perfect.

I can't help myself. I lean in closer.

I can feel how hard her heart is beating as I kiss her, savoring every fucking second of her lips against mine before I force myself to pull away.

She has this glazed over look in her eyes as she sits back in her car. Adorable. I fucking love this girl. All mine.

I tell her goodnight, but I don't even think she even hears me as she drives home. I smile my entire way to her house. I finally kissed her. About fucking time. Her lips were so fucking soft. And that whimper when I pulled away... Fuck. I could've fucked her right against her car. Sounded so fucking sweet...

I watched as she stepped out of her bedroom, only wearing some panties and a t shirt. Looking so fucking edible. She grabbed herself a glass of water before heading back up to bed. Goodnight doll.

About 30 minutes later, I make my way up to her room. There she is... my fucking angel. I walk over to her, tracing over her pretty face before placing some kisses all over her, then one on her lips... just to feel them again...

I come to lay down next to her, and her sleeping body automatically curls up into my arms. Like it's second nature.

I wrap my arms around her, letting her sink deeper into my warmth. I got you baby. I'll never let anything happen to you.

My fingers glide up the back of her t shirt, raking my fingers down her back, causing her to let out a sleepy hum. My other hand rests on her hip, my fingers brushing over her ass softly. I press a kiss to her head, thinking of what it would be like when she's finally mine. Like a fucking dream.

Maybe I should just ask her out...Be the normal, thoughtful kind of guy that she needs.And never fucking let her find out the lengths I've gone for her.I want her to feel safe in my arms, not scared.I'd never harm her.

I wish I knew what happened with that guy in the bar earlier.Sam.I can't imagine what would ever bring someone to hurt such a perfect fucking human.Fucking scum.

I guess it's not important.Seeing as I'll make sure he can never hurt my girl again.Never.

But I'll enjoy my night with her first, making sure she's safe and comfortable after everything.She'll always be my priority.As the sun comes up, I kiss her pretty lips one last time before I leave.

I have someone to go handle.Anything for you doll.

# Chapter 19- Hailey

I curl up into his arms the second he lays down beside me. I just needed him to hold me.

I hummed softly as his fingers trace up my back, his other hand finding my ass. Typical. I grin.

I don't have the energy to do anything else besides fall asleep in this moment, just feeling safe and warm in his arms. I know he'll watch over me.

•••

I get up out of bed the next day, smiling as I smell him on my sheets. I have a nice slow morning, cooking myself a big breakfast, then getting around to clean up my place. Ryder isn't here so I try and enjoy my day off by watching one of my favorite movies.

Feeling bored after, I change into some workout clothes and head down to the gym for a few hours. No sign of his huge self here either.

•••

Happy with a good workout in, I head back home, noticing he hasn't come back yet. I just shrug it off, stepping into a hot shower. He can't be here all the time.

I take my time washing my hair and body before getting out, dressing in some comfortable clothes. As I'm doing my hair, I hear a loud crash come from downstairs. Ryder? I stay in my room for a minute, hearing loud footsteps. This doesn't sound like him. He's too careful.

Panic starts to set in as my breathing becomes harder. Shit. Please be him. Please be him. I grab my phone, my finger hovering over his contact. Shaking. Fuck it. I press dial.

"Hey-"

"Are you in my house right now?" I cut him off, speaking softly. I try to hide how fucking shaky my voice is right now.

"No- why would I-" I cut him off again

"Ryder- are you in my house right now" I ask again, my voice dead fucking serious this time. Please say yes.

"No doll-" I hear another sound come from downstairs.

"Cause there's somebody in my house right now Ryder." I get out, barely a whisper.

He's silent for a moment.

"Fuck" he grits out. "I'm coming baby. Can you lock yourself in your bathroom baby? I'm coming" he says quickly, panic in his tone.

"Yes" I tell him, locking myself in my bathroom, trying to take deep breaths. "Please hurry" I get out.

"I'm coming as fast as I can doll. Don't hang up on me okay. I'll be there in just a few minutes" he reassures me, cursing.

"Okay" I say softly, hearing another noise downstairs.

"I'm almost there doll. Stay there for me. Fuck." He curses, and I sit back in my bathtub, trying to calm myself down.He's coming.He won't let anything happen to you.

"I'm pulling up now. Don't fucking open that bathroom door for anyone but me alright? You hear me?" He says breathlessly

"I understand Ryder" I tell himThen the call disconnects.No no no.

Moments later I hear a loud crash from downstairs, holding my breath.I can hear voices. Loud noises.Then a gunshot.

Nothing. I hear nothing.I close my eyes, curling up into my legs as I hope and pray he's okay.Please be okay.

Tears well up in my eyes as I wait. It's all I can fucking do.He told me to stay put.I hear soft footsteps. They're getting closer.The tears begin to fall down my cheeks.Please be him.Please god be him.

It's silent for a moment before there's a soft knock on my bathroom door."It's me doll. I'm here. It's okay" I let out a sob at his voice.I jump up out of the tub, rushing to open the door.Before he could say anything, I crash into him, wrapping my arms around him as tears stream down, wetting his shirt.

"I've got you doll, you're okay. I've got you now." He whispers softly into my hair, stroking it gently.I stay like this for god knows how long.Till my tears have stopped and my breathing comes back to normal.He just keeps whispering reassuring words into my ear, holding me tight.

"Thank you" I mumble into his chest, clutching him tightly.

"Of course doll. I'm so fucking sorry. So fucking sorry." He says over and over again. He sounds so guilty.

I look up at him. "It's not your fault" I smile softly "You were the one who came. Who saved me." I tell him, and he just squeezes me tighter.

He presses a kiss to my head, cupping my cheeks as he looks down at me. "Don't go downstairs yet, okay?" He says gently. My eyebrows furrowed in confusion. "Why?" "I don't want you to see." He tells me, brushing his thumb against my cheek.

"Someone was trying to rob you. I know some people that are coming to clean everything up soon. You don't need to see everything." He explains softly.

I nod softly. "What do you need? Water? Food? Anything." He asks me.

"Just hold me please" I tell him. He nods, leading us over to my bed.

When he lays down, I come to straddle his lap, wrapping my arms around his neck as I rest my head on his shoulder. I can tell I caught him off guard at first, but he quickly wraps him arms around me, pulling me flush against his chest.

He strokes my back soothingly for a while and I find my fingers playing with the hair at the nape of his neck. He smells so good. He occasionally places a kiss or two on my shoulder, and I smile at the feeling. This is exactly where I need to be. In his arms. Where no one can hurt me.

I close my eyes, just breathing in his scent as my body relaxes. I hear movement downstairs, but Ryder assures me those are just his "friends" cleaning up the mess. He killed someone for me. To protect me.

I knew nobody else would ever care about me as much as he did. And that made me smile.

"Hey doll?" He asks softly "Mmhm?" I mumble against his chest "Why did you think I was in your house when you called me?" He asks carefully

I pause for a moment.

"How did you know how to get to my house so quickly?"

# Chapter 20- Ryder

I send Sam's plate number to a buddy who owes me a favor. It's not long before I get his location, gathering my things before heading off to find him. This was personal.

He wasn't too far away which was good. I could be back to my girl soon.

His face when I showed up at his door was priceless. Even better when I beat the shit out of him for grabbing my angel. And best of all when I put a bullet in his stupid brain. He'll never get to my girl again.

I'm on my way back when I hear my phone ring, answering it quickly. Could be her.

I'm so happy to hear her voice until I notice how panicked she sounds. My heart fucking drops "Are you in my house right now?" Oh fuck.

I tell her no- actually being honest at the moment. Then she asks me again. It's then I know something is wrong. I tell her no again- and she stops me.

"Cause there's somebody in my house right now Ryder." Fuck. Fuck. Fuck. The one time I'm not there to protect her.

I'm driving so fucking fast towards her the other cars look like they're standing still."I'm coming baby. Can you lock yourself in your bathroom baby? I'm coming"I've never been so scared in my life.

When she begs me to hurry in a desperate voice my fucking heart breaks.If anything happens to her I'll never forgive myself.I should've been there.

I keep trying to reassure her, not even processing the words that are leaving my mouth as I get to her as fast as I can.I turn down her street, unbuckling as I pull into her drive.

"I'm pulling up now. Don't fucking open that bathroom door for anyone but me alright? You hear me?" I say, opening my car door, hand reaching for my gun."I understand Ryder"As soon as I hear that. I end the call.I'm coming baby.

I kick open the front door as my eyes set on some man in a black hoodie, a mask covering half of his face.He turns to me startled, nearly dropping the tv out of his hands.This little fucker.Stealing from my girl.

I point my gun at him and he freezes."Man- I'll leave. I didn't even take anything yet. I'll leave it all here-"Shoot.

He falls down to the ground, his blood seeping into her pretty rug.Sorry doll.I call a team of people that can clean the body up and fix up the house for her.I didn't want her to see this.To see him.

I head upstairs quickly, approaching her bathroom door.I take a deep breath.I knock."It's me doll. I'm here. It's okay" I say softly.Seconds later, the door is thrown open and she practically jumps onto me.She sobs softly into my chest as I wrap my arms around her tightly, trying to comfort her in any way I could.

I rub her back softly, whispering soothing words to her, telling her she's safe now. My girl must have been so scared. And I wasn't there to protect her. It's all my fucking fault.

"Thank you" she says softly Thank you? Of course I'd fucking come.

I just apologize to her. Over and over. I'm so sorry doll.

"You were the one who came. Who saved me." She tells me, looking up into my eyes. She's so fucking perfect. Knows exactly what to say. I just hold her tighter, wishing this girl knew that she was my entire fucking world.

"Don't go downstairs okay?" I tell her, explaining that I'll have some people come by and fix everything up for her. I just want her to be able to relax. Not deal with any of that shit. I just wanted to be there for her.

"What do you need? Water? Food? Anything." I ask her

"Just hold me please" she says God, this girl couldn't be more perfect if she tried.

I nod, leading her over to the bed where she'd be more comfortable. I sit back, surprised when she plops herself in my lap, straddling me. I feel her hands come around my neck, her head resting on my shoulder.

I soon move to wrap my arms around her, pulling her tight against me. This is perfect.

I feel her body relax in my arms, her eyes closing for a moment. Then I realize something.

She asked if I was in her house. Me.

She knows. But she couldn't... she wouldn't let me hold her if she knew. She'd be scared.

I take a deep breath."Hey doll?""Mmhm" she mumbles"Why did you think I was in your house when you called me?" I ask carefully

She just lies there for a moment. My heart is fucking racing.I hope she can't feel it.

"How did you know how to get to my house so quickly?" She replies calmly

Touché doll.

I grin to myself as she nuzzles closer into the crook of my neck."You know." I say out loud, looking down curiously at my precious girl.She knows.How?And why is she okay with it?

She leans up slightly to face me, a soft smirk on her lips."Know what Ryder?" She asks sweetlyYou little fucking tease. I grin widely.

"Don't play games with me doll" I tell her, gripping her hips as I pull her closer to me.Her smirk just widens.My pretty girl figured me out.So fucking smart.

"You started it" she grins"Yeah?""You're not a very good stalker you know ..." she teases.

I can't fucking believe this."How long did you know?" I ask her, gaping at her in astonishment."The past three months... how long have you been watching me?" She questions."Around 4..." I smile.My observant girl...

"I don't understand... you're not upset?" I ask her, genuinely confused. But also excited.She's okay with me.

She just shrugs, "I was bothered a bit at first... but I grew to like it..." she explains with a smile.My girl.Fucking crazy in the same way I am.Made for me.

# Chapter 21- Hailey

------------------------------------------------

I grin as his hands grip my hips tighter.He just looks at me with such curiosity... admiration.I wonder what's going through his head right now.

"Hmm so you've just known this whole time yeah? Did you enjoy yourself doll? Toying with me?" He asks with a smirk.I can tell he's not mad. More intrigued.well, you underestimated me baby.

"I had my fun at some points..." I grin, leaning closer"Don't act like you didn't enjoy every second of it" I say softly.His grip tightens.He smiles.

His hands leave my hips, coming up to cup my face."So damn perfect for me." He mumbles, bringing me closer to him.His lips just brush against mine and shivers run over my body.I love how me makes me feel.So fucking good. Like his.

He finally kisses me, his hand threading into my scalp to keep me in place as he kisses the fuck out of me.If I was standing, I think my knees would have caved in.

I gasp softly as his tongue slips into my mouth, fogging my mind.I can't even think about anything else that happened.Just him.This.

I pull back when he finally releases me, breathless. I can feel how hot my cheeks are and I see him smirk widely at the sight.

"So fucking sweet" he mumbles.

I can fucking feel how hard he is beneath me, and it's driving me mad.I move my hips slowly against him, my eyes closing at the friction.His hands quickly grab my hips, holding me still.There's this dark look in his eyes as he stares at me.I fucking love it.

"Dangerous fucking move doll" he grits out.I just grin."What's wrong with that hm?" I tease"Because..." he begins"Right now you need to relax... process everything. I don't want you to do anything you'll regret." He says, looking me in my eyes.

Then he leans forward, his lips brushing just over the shell of my ear."And, there's about five men downstairs right now cleaning up that I'd have to kill for hearing your pretty fucking moans""You wouldn't want that right love?" He taunts.FuckI've never been so turned on in my life.I shake my head no.

"That's right. Be a good girl for me and stay still then." He smiles

I just nod.

"Ryder?" I ask softlyHe hums for me to continue, his thumbs rubbing over my hips softly."Why did you start watching me?" I ask slowly.This is all I've wanted to know for months.

"It's simple.""I knew you were made for me. Made to be mine. I just felt it." He tells me, nothing but truth in his eyes.I smile so fucking wide.Made for him.And he's made for me.

He brushes the curls out of my face, cupping my cheek."I'd fucking do anything for you doll. Kill for you. You know that?" He asks meMy heart pounds in my chest."Yes" I get out softly

"Do I scare you baby?" He asks, a soft smirk on his lips.I wait for a moment. Thinking.

"You make my nervous. But I know you'd never really hurt me. So no. You don't scare me" I tell him.His other hand comes to my face as well, bringing me closer so I can see how serious he is.

"Good. Because I want you to know you're the most important fucking thing in the world to me. Fucking perfect to me." My heart flutters.Why does he have to say things like that?Makes me want to marry this man.

"Do you understand me?" He asks gently"Yes" I nod softly"I want to hear you say it. Tell me you're perfect"God. This man."I'm perfect..." I tell him softly

He smiles"That's right. Such a good fucking girl" I have to fight the urge to squirm at his fucking words, my body feeling all too hot at the moment.Why is he so damn good at this.

He just presses another kiss to my lips, running his hands over my thighs.His phone light up with a message, and he glances at it before looking back up at me."They're all done doll. You want to do downstairs? Eat something?" I smile, nodding softly.

"They should've fixed your door with a better deadbolt for you, and cleaned up everything. There might be a few things damaged though, alright?" He explains smoothly."I'll help you replace anything you want." He says, helping me off his lap.

"Okay" I smile, taking his hand as he leads me downstairs.I look around, most things looking in place.There's a few small things missing but nothing important.It's better than I thought honestly."They did a good job. I can hardly tell" I say to Ryder.

"Good. I'm glad you're happy with it." He grins, leading me over to the kitchen."Hungry?""Starving." I sigh"Well I can't have my girl going hungry now can I?" He grins, picking me up and setting me on the kitchen counter easily.Hot.

I laugh softly as he kisses my face all over, turning around to open my fridge."What do you want doll? I'll make you something" Hmmm."Pasta?" I ask him"Anything you want doll."

I watch him as he puts some pasta in a pot to boil, starting to make a sauce for in.The muscles of his back strain against his shirt as he works, and I bite my lip, distracted.God he looks too good."You staring at me doll?" he says, not even turning around to look at me.He just knew.

"Yeah" I grinHe turns around with a smirk."Thought that was my job love" he winks at me, making me laugh.

I hop off the counter, walking over to him."What? I can't stare at you?" I ask, teasing."You can stare at me all you want doll. I'm all yours."I'm speechless as he grabs my waist, pulling me in for a kiss.All mine

# Chaper 22- Ryder

------

I could feel her pretty eyes on me while I was cooking for her.Well this is a fun turn of events

My grin widens when she comes over to approach me, hearing her soft footsteps.I turn to face her when she comes closer.

"What? I can't stare at you?" She asks me, a teasing smile on her lips.My little vixen. "You can stare at me all you want doll. I'm all yours." I tell her, reaching out to grab her waist so I can pull her closer.

You have no idea how badly I'm wrapped around your finger love.

I lean down, pressing a kiss to her plump lips.My hands run down to her lower back, pulling her as close to me as possible.I wanted to have every fucking inch of her against me.Her hands thread into my scalp and it feels so good i practically groan into her mouth.Such a little temptress.

I finally break away, grinning down at her flushed face as she catches her breath.I pick her up again, sitting her on the counter beside the stove so I can look at her perfect self while I finish cooking.I add the pasta to the sauce, smiling as I hear her stomach growl, causing her to grow even more embarrassed."Hungry doll?" I teaseI just wanted to see her pretty cheeks red.

I smile as I hand her a bowl, laughing as she quickly digs in. "Wow- this is good" she mumbles, mouth full of pasta."What? Didn't think I could cook?" I ask grinning

I sit there, eating my own as I watch her in admiration.I've never seen someone devour food so damn quickly...Fucking love this woman.

When she's finished, I take her bowl, pressing a kiss to her lips."I'll clean this up. Why don't you go shower so you feel better hm?" I say, brushing the hair out of her face."That sounds so good right now" she sighs."Good. I'll take care of this" "Ryder?" She looks up at me sweetly."Yeah doll?""Will you stay with me tonight?"Oh pretty girl."Was going to whether you wanted me to or not" I tell her with a grin.

She smiles, walking upstairs to her bedroom.I'll be there soon doll.I do all the dishes, making sure to clean up the whole kitchen while I'm here.

I fucking loved just taking care of her.Just being here with her.My perfect girl.

I head upstairs, hearing her shower turn off.I lie back on her bed, waiting for her to come out.When she does, I'm not fucking disappointed.

She's in that little silk robe she teased me in that one night, her curls pulled up out of her face.Fucking mesmerizing.All fucking mine.She just gives me an innocent little smile like she has no idea what she's doing with me.

She grabs her bottle of coconut lotion as I stand up, coming behind her.She smells so damn good. "Let me doll. Please." I say, taking the bottle from her.

She nods softly, and I place my hand on her lower back, guiding her to her bed. She grins as I have her sit back on the soft covers, getting some lotion on my hands before leaning down and beginning to rub it into her arms.

I take my time, loving the feeling of her skin against my hands. The way she looks at me. Everything. I work my way down to her hands, massaging them for a few minutes before placing a kiss on each one. My girl deserved the fucking best treatment and I intend to give her it.

I kneel down in front of her, taking one of her smooth legs into my hold. She leans back onto her elbows, watching me with these hazy eyes that make my dick hard. God. Take a deep breath. I start massaging her foot with the lotion, making my way up to her calf, leaving a trail of kisses as I go. I do the same to the other leg before moving to her thighs. Her sexy fucking thighs.

They fucking glow as I rub the lotion into her skin, my hands slowly making their way higher. At this point I can tell she's not wearing anything under the robe and it's driving me fucking mad.

I lean down, leaving kisses up her thighs that have her whining. Sounds too fucking good. I'm still not convinced this isn't an amazing fucking dream. I bite down into the soft flesh, making her gasp. Couldn't help myself

"Just a taste doll. I need to." I say, looking up at her. I give her a moment to push me away, praying she doesn't. She just looks down at me with those pretty eyes that seem to be begging for more.

"Ryder" she whimpersFucking begging.

I can't fucking wait anymore. I spread her thighs, groaning at the sight of her. She's so fucking wet. Practically dripping.

My dick is so hard it's painful. But that doesn't matter to me. It's all her.

I grin widely as I pull her hips to the edge of the mattress, spreading her legs wider."This all for me doll? Hm? Tell me." I look up at her, fucking panting with need."Yes. All for you" she whines softly."Good girl. So fuckin good." I say before diving into her pretty pussy.

I drag my tongue slowly from her entrance to her clit, groaning at the taste of her.Even better than I remember.

I circle my tongue around her slit, loving the way her whines and pleads fill my ears.Fucking desperate for me. Just how I want her.

"Tastes so damn good" i mumble, her hands threading into my hair.There you go doll.

I move her thighs to settle on each of my shoulders, getting her as close as I possibly can.

I start to move my tongue faster, holding her hips down against the mattress as I fucking devour her.I can't ever get enough of this.Her taste. Her sounds. The way she feels.

I flick my tongue over her clit as her back arches up off of her mattress, her moans getting louder.I need this.Fucking crave this more than anything.I go faster, my grip on her hips tightening as I can tell she's getting close, her hips trying to wiggle away from me.I'm not done with you yet doll.

"Ryder- oh fuck"

I eat her pussy like I'm starving.I fucking am.

She cries out in pleasure as her legs start to shake, pushing me to keep going.I watch as her stomach caves in, and she gasps out a moan, cumming on my tongue like the good fucking girl she is.So damn perfect.I keep going, prolonging this as long as I can as she mumbles my name over and over again.I've got you doll.

My eyes study her body's every movement and tremor, the beautiful way her thighs clench around my head...I make sure to get every last fucking drop of her onto my tongue before coming up.I need this. Over and over again.

"You taste so fucking addictive you know that doll?" I grin.Her eyes flutter open to meet mine, a smile playing on her lip."Shame, I guess I'm stuck with you now" she says, pulling me closer.I lean down, kissing her perfect lips.

"You already were doll. Can't get rid of me."I lay back on her bed with the biggest smirk.

"Now how about you sit your pretty ass on my face so I can make my girl cum again?"

# Chapter 23- Hailey

"I can't- oh my god-" I moan, cumming for the third time on this man's face tonight. My fingers were gripping the headboard so hard I worried it would break. I was seriously going to pass out soon.

I kept trying to pull away, wanting to do something for him. I felt bad. But he just kept mumbling how he wasn't finished yet, coaxing me through another orgasm. Nobody has even made me feel anywhere close to this good.

He pulls away finally, giving me a moment to breathe. My eyes still closed tightly. "Look at me pretty girl" he tells me, his hands rubbing up my thighs. I look down. The lower half of his face is covered in my release, a proud smirk curving on his lips. God he's hot.

"That's it. Eyes on me. Did so fucking good for me." He praises and I can feel my cheeks flaming red. I can't take him talking to me like this. Does things to me that I can't even explain. I keep my eyes on him, leaning against my headboard. One of his hands holds my waist while the other reaches up to cup my face. "Tired doll?" I nod my head quickly. Another orgasm would kill me. I swear.

He gives me a knowing grin before lifting me off him, setting me down on my back as he gets up off the bed.He returns a minute later from my bathroom with a washcloth, cleaning me up silently.I just lie there in shock.He throws the towel in the laundry before joining me, turning off my lamp."Sleep doll. I've got you" he says softly, pulling me into his warm body.

I'm so fucking exhausted.I rest my head on his chest, feeling his fingers lightly play with my hair.And just like that, I'm out. Drifting into the sweetest sleep, feeling so utterly satisfied.

•••

I wake up the next morning, feeling his arms wrapped around me tightly.I glance up at him, noticing he's still sleeping.

I slowly try and wiggle out of his hold, not wanting to wake him, but his grip just gets tighter on me.Big clingy idiot.I wait a few more minutes before trying again, his grip on me becoming painfully tight as a frown forms on his face.

"No" he mumbles softlyI roll my eyes."I just want to go to the bathroom..." I groan, squirming away from him.

"Be quick" he sighs, loosening his grip on me so I can finally get up.A few minutes later, he walks into the bathroom with a grumpy look on his face.He comes behind me as I'm doing my hair, wrapping his arms around me."I told you to be quick" he mumbles in my ear, pulling me back against him.

"You're a fucking caveman, you know that?" I sigh, meeting his eyes in the mirror.He just grins"You like it" he tells meNot entirely wrong there...

Once I get dressed, he insists on feeding me, practically dragging me do wnstairs."I'll make something for us" I tell him."You wanna cook for me doll?" He smirks"Don't let it go to your head" "Too late" he smiles, kissing me on my cheek before finally letting me go.

He leans back on the kitchen counter beside me, staring as I cook.His eyes follow up the bare skin of my legs before reaching my shorts, licking his lips.I'm flipping pancakes as he comes behind me, holding onto my hips while trailing kisses down my neck and onto my shoulder.Flashbacks of last night fill my mind.My legs fucking trembling at how good it felt.Stop it.

"You're being distracting." I tell him, nudging him off me.He laughs, giving me one last kiss on my neck before backing off."That's the point doll"

I roll my eyes at him, handing him a plate."Thanks love" he smiles, walking around to take a seat at my kitchen table.I go to take to seat next to him, but he grabs me, pulling me onto his lap.

"You're insatiable..." I tell him, but I can't help the grin that comes to my face."Damn right I am when it comes to you."I seriously can't ever be annoyed with him.Not when he talks to me like that.

We eat together, one of his hands rubbing over my thigh as he shoves bites of pancakes in his mouth.

We spend most of the day curled up on the couch together, and I have to swat his hand away from going beneath my clothes every 5 minutes.Man seriously can't help himself.

•••

"Come on... I have to go to work soon. Let me go get ready" I pleaded, trying to get him to let me out of his hold."You know, now that you're mine, you don't have to work unless you want to. I'd happily take care of you angel." he tells me.He's too perfect. I can't stand it.

I just wanted to fuck with him. Make him flustered like he does with me.

"And who said I was yours, hm?" I ask with a smirk. His smile immediately drops and his eyes darken. Oh shit... He looks fucking deadly. It's turning me on.

"You don't think you're mine huh?" He arches a brow at me, his grip tightening around me. I shake my head no, too excited to even speak.

Oh I'm definitely going to push him over the edge.

He stands up, carrying me with him back to my bedroom, throwing me on the bed. I watch as he leans down over me, my heart pounding at the way he looks down at me. Fucking hot.

He gets on top of me, his arms on either side as he cages me in. He looks like a damn predator catching his prey. I like it.

One of his hands comes to my thigh, heading up to grip my waist. "Sure seemed like mine when you were making a fucking mess on my face last night huh?" He says, looking directly into my eyes.

I can't stop the whimper that leaves my throat. Fuck.

"You need me to show you who you belong to doll? A reminder?" He tsks, leaning closer. I nod, unable to form words. Show me.

(a/n- haha I know I'm the worst)

# Chapter 24- Ryder

This little fucking brat.Saying she's not mine.Oh baby you have no idea what you've done. I'll make sure she has no fucking doubt who she belongs to.I'll fucking imprint it in her brain so that she never forgets it.All. Fucking. Mine.

I lean over her, pinning her down against the mattress so she has nowhere to run.Her eyes look scared. But I can tell she's doing this on purpose.Fucking provoking me.You shouldn't poke the bear doll.

"You need me to show you who you belong to doll? A reminder?" I taunt, my smirk growing as she squirms beneath my touch.She nods.Good girl.

I grip her jaw, leaning down to kiss her harshly. She moans softly into my mouth as my hands glide over her body, my thumb brushing over one of her hardened nipples through her tank top.Fucking desperate.

I pull back, taking the flimsy piece of fabric off.Grabbing her wrists, I pin her hands to the mattress with one hand, my lips dragging down between her breasts as she whines softly.

I take one of her nipples into my mouth, sucking as my free hand massages her other breast.Her skin feels so damn soft against my touch.

She arches her back, pushing her tits further into my face."So fucking needy hm?" I tease, switching to the other breast.

I then drag her shorts off, noticing she doesn't have any panties on."No panties huh doll? Were you just waiting for me to play with your pretty pussy again?" I grin, my thumb gliding up her wet folds before circling over her clit.She lets out the prettiest fucking gasp.She's the most perfect thing I've ever seen.

"You look so fuckin pretty for me." I tell her, kissing around her breasts as my thumb circles her sensitive bundle of nerves.She lets out these small moans, biting her lip to keep herself quiet.Oh baby, don't do that."Let me hear you doll. Show me how good I make you feel" I tell her.

She looks up at me, her cheeks flushed and her eyes dark and stormy.She's trying to be disobedient but she can't help the way her perfect body responds to me.I fucking love that.

She releases her bottom lip, it all puffy and red as she moans for me, her head tilting back."Please... more" she gasps outSo fucking pretty.But I wasn't fucking done playing with her.She needed to learn who she belongs to.

"Hm, what do you want pretty girl? You want my cock doll?" I ask her teasingly.She nods so desperately, looking up at me with those sexy little fuck me eyes.Not so fast doll.

"Use your words baby. Tell me what you want yeah?" I smirk, slowing my thumb against her clit just to watch her beg for more.You started this doll."Please Ryder... please fuck me" she begsFuck that sounds so damn good.I've got you doll.

I smirk as I throw my shirt over my head, unbuttoning my pants so that I can take my cock out.She leans up, watching me with this needy look in her eyes. So fuckin sexy.I'm already rock hard for her, her lips parting as she looks down at my solid length.That's right baby."You want my cock in you doll? That what you need?" I ask, hovering over her once again.

"Yes. Yes- please" she gasps out, her eyes on me."Stay still for me doll. Don't you dare move" I tell her and she nods quickly."Good girl, that's it."I rub my cock against her wet pussy, closing my eyes at the feeling.Not yet."Tell me this fucking pussy is mine angel. Tell me who the fuck you belong to." I say roughly, gliding my cock back and forth against her pussy, making her whimper.

"Yours. I'm all yours- please Ryder" she moans, her hips lifting in search of more.That's what I wanted to hear doll.

"Good fucking girl. All mine" I grit out, lining up with her entrance.I slowly push inside, gripping onto her hips as her legs wrap around me.So fucking tight. So perfect.She chokes out a gasp, her eyes shutting as she winces softly."Relax for me baby. You can take it. So fucking good." I tell her, my thumb coming to rub her clit softly to help her relax.She'll take every fucking inch of me.

I let out a deep groan as I sink fully inside her, her mouth dropping open as her eyes remain closed tightly."Open your eyes love. Watch me fuck your pretty little pussy yeah? Eyes on me." I tell her, grinning as her eyes open to meet mine.She looks so fucking needy.All for me.

"That's it baby" I tell her, slowly pulling back before thrusting inside her again.She lets out a moan, her pussy clenching around me.Fuck. So fucking good.I start to fuck her faster, her hands gripping onto me tightly as her moans get louder.

"Fuck- Ryder..." she moans, her hips lifting to meet each of my thrusts.I can feel her soft breathing and gasps against my skin, kissing her lips.So fucking perfect for me.

"That's right baby. Feel how deep I am in that tight pussy of yours? So fucking good for me doll" I say, praising her before dipping down to kiss over her neck.

Her head falls back in pleasure, and I move her legs to my shoulders, letting me get even deeper as she cries out for more."Take my fucking cock doll. Just like that" I groan, feeling her pussy tighten around me.I wanted to feel her cum around my cock so fucking desperately.

"Ryder I-" she gasps"I know doll, I know. Let go for me gorgeous" I encourage her as I rub her clit with my thumb, feeling her body tense up.That's it love. "Cum for me angel" I tell her, fucking her pussy faster.She lets out a broken moan as she cums, her nails digging deep into my arms.I couldn't even bother to care, all I can fucking feel is the way her pussy clenches around me right now."Fuck- that's it. Such a good girl, cumming for me" I groan, feeling my own release coming soon.

I fuck her through her orgasm, gripping onto her shaky body as I hold back as long as I can.Her sweet moans and whimpers send me over the edge as I cum deep inside her, loving the soft gasp that leaves her lips.After a few last thrusts, I pull back, looking down at this perfect woman in my arms.

"All fucking mine yeah?" I get out, fucking breathless."All yours"

# Chapter 25- Hailey

Blood rushes to my head as I feel his cock deep inside me.I can barely keep my eyes open, but the way he looks down at me is so fucking hot I can't look away.

I'm a moaning mess as I grip onto his arms, feeling the muscles flexing under my hold.Oh my god.

I can feel my entire body moving with each of his hard thrusts.

"That's right baby. Feel how deep I am in that tight pussy of yours? So fucking good for me baby" he gets out in a rough voice that makes my pussy clench.He's gonna make me cum if he keeps talking to me this this...Fucking me like this.

His large body hovers over mine, every muscle seeming to flex and bulge with his movements.Sweat glides down the planes of his chest, his grip on me so fucking possessive.

This was so worth the begging.I needed to provoke him more often if this is what happens to me...

I feel his lips on my neck. Sucking and marking the skin as he fucks me harder. Faster.I could feel my stomach tightening, my orgasm approaching quickly.It's like he knows exactly how to play my body to his will.

"I know doll, I know. Let go for me gorgeous" he groans softly, his thumb returning to rub my clit.My breathing is ragged as he stares down at me with so much intensity.

My legs tighten around him, my body arching up off the mattress as I cum for him, craving more of this feeling. Of him.My mind goes blank as he keeps fucking me roughly, head dizzy as I feel him cum deep inside me.My body feels like it's on fire.In the best way

He hovers over me, his hand moving to brush away the curls that are stuck to my face, grinning."All fucking mine yeah?"I smirk.Fucking possessive bastard."All yours" I tell him.

"How about you go call out of work for tonight... tell them you're sick... or better yet, immobile" he teases.I roll my eyes at his cockiness."Don't make me fuck that attitude out of you doll" he calls out, grabbing a washcloth from the bathroom.

I laugh softly as he hands me my phone, waiting for me to call in.Fine.If I was being honest I wanted to stay here and get fucked again anyways.

After I hang up the phone, I toss it aside.Ryder starts kissing up my still naked body, grinning widely."Let's go take a shower baby..." he whispers in my ear."I want to clean you up before I ruin your pretty body all over again" he continuesI can feel my cheeks flaming red.This man needs to stop constantly turning me on.He pulls me up into his arms, carrying me into my bathroom.

Kissing me on my shoulder, he sets me down in front of the mirror before turning to start the shower.

He comes back to me, wrapping his arms around my waist from behind as he looks over my body in the reflection.

He admires the many marks he left on me with a grin, tracing his fingers over them softly."So fucking pretty" he mumbles against my neck.This man is a dream.

I step into the shower and he laughs as he drags me under the water with him.His fingers move to brush my wet hair out of my face, kissing me.

I feel his hands drag down my back, cupping my ass tightly with both hands.He raises one of his hands, bringing it back down to smack my ass. Hard."Ow-" I whine softly, trying to hide my grin.

"That's for trying to say you're not mine" he smirks, rubbing his hand over my ass softly to soothe the sting."Hmm" I grin, my hands going up his chest, feeling over his muscles.Love a big strong man that could just pick me up and fuck me...

He grabs my coconut body wash, squirting some on his hands before leaning down, rubbing it into my body.I sigh softly at the feeling, his hands all over me.He massages my tits with a grin before moving down to my waist.

He then kneels down in front of me as he moves to my ass, taking extra time there before going down my legs.He stands up, pulling me against him before he turns us around, letting the water rush over my body as he leans in.He inhales my skin deeply, nearly groaning.Struggling baby?

"I fucking love the smell of you. So fucking sweet" he tells me, gripping my jaw to look up at him.I smile."I like how you smell to. Deep. Manly." I smile."Oh yeah doll?""Mmhm. I used to smell you on my sheets when you would leave in the morning" He smirks.

"You knew I came in while you slept too then huh? Little fuckin tease" he says, tracing over my jawline lightly.Shivers."I was awake sometimes... I'd pretend to be asleep." I grinNot as stupid as you thought hm?

"So you knew what you were doing when you'd curl your little body up in my arms....Didn't even say anything when I'd come into your work... just torturing me for fun huh?" He tsks.

"Well..." I trace my fingers down his abdomen"I wasn't the one stalking someone... but I had to have a little fun." "And we both know you enjoyed it too..." I smirk.He pulls me closer, my wet body flush against his.

"So... that night when you touched yourself... you knew I was there huh? Putting on a show for me doll?" He smirks, gripping my ass.I nod softly." And I was awake when you came in and tasted me on my fingers later that night too..." I tease and he groans.

"You have no idea how painful it was for me to hold myself back watching you like that...My pretty little tease..." he taunts, looking down at me.I grin, shrugging"I should fuck you again for being such a fucking temptress... playing with your pussy while you knew I was watching..." he trails offI bite my lip, hiding a smirk.

I feel his hand slip between my thighs, his fingers rubbing along my slit. "Did you cum for me that night? Did knowing I was watching turn you on?" He teases, rubbing my clit."Yes" I whimper, my legs feeling weak.

He smirks, wrapping his other arm around my waist so that he's supporting my weight."That's alright doll. I can make up for all that lost time over these past few months... fuck this pussy of yours any time I want."

I moan softly at his words, his fingers moving quicker."You'd let me fuck you whenever I want, isn't that right doll?" He grits out in my ear and damn if this wasn't making my pussy soaking wet.

"Yes sir" I moan, remembering his reaction to me calling him that weeks ago.He lets out a loud groan of approval, slipping two fingers inside me as I gasp out."That's it, such a good fucking girl for me yeah? All mine." He says, pumping his fingers in and out of me quickly.I can feel his hot breath against my ear, making my shiver.

I can feel my orgasm already coming, holding onto his shoulders as I rest my head against him.He curls his fingers in just the right way, his palm rubbing against my clit as he goes faster.So fucking good.

"Cum for me doll, just like that" he groansMy walls clench against his fingers as my body follows his order, my moans muffled into his chest.He holds me up as my knees give in, praising me and telling me how good I'm doing.I need this man inside me. Now.

# Chapter 26- Ryder

I memorized every moan that left her lips. The spots that my fingers hit that make her shutter. I was going to learn every little response of her body to the point where I knew it better than she did.

The way her pussy clenched around my fingers had my cock throbbing against her stomach. I fucking needed her all the time. I couldn't get enoughHer body was so warm against mine, her pretty face pressed firmly against my skin.

As she rode out her orgasm, her moans and whimpers were muffled against my chest. I could feel the vibrations of her throat against me.

The steam from the shower filled the room as I guided her to stand back up, making sure she was steady on her feet.

I came up behind her, grabbing her hands and placing them against the glass wall. "You look so damn good cumming for me..." I whisper into her ear.

She whimpers as my hand pushes down on her lower back, making her arch for me. I grin, my hands gliding over her waist and down to her hips. She pushes them back towards me eagerly. "Ryder..." Needy girl.

She looks back over her shoulder at me, biting down on her lower lip. She looks so good like this...Bent over for me, drunk on pleasure.

"Patience doll... you gonna be a good girl for me now?" I taunt, pressing my hard cock against her ass. "Yes-" she whines I tsk "Yes what doll?" I smirk "Yes sir." God I love that.

I thrust inside her all at once, and she cries out. "Oh my god- fuck" I hold her steady as I start fucking into her tight little pussy, groaning at how wet and hot she is.

I reach one of my hands beneath her, grasping one of her breasts in my hand as I fuck her.

"So fucking perfect for me yeah? God- you're so damn tight" I groan softly She whines and moans, her hand prints left against the fogged up glass. I pinch her nipple harshly before I let my hand glide up to her throat.

I feel her gulp around my hand, her pulse racing beneath my fingertips .Drops of water fell down her curves, tracing the beautiful skin beneath me. Fucking mesmerizing

I wrap my hand around the front of her neck, pulling her body up so that her back is arched against my front. She feels so damn good.

My other hand hooks along her waist, holding her up as I fuck her deep and fast. My hand squeezes the sides of her pretty throat, restricting the blood flow. She moans louder for me.

"You like that doll? You gonna cum for me? Cum on my cock baby." I get out breathlessly. She lets out a broken gasp, her body trembling as she cums for me. "That's it... so fucking pretty" I groan out

My thrusts get faster, feeling her pussy clenching around me.Fuckin heavenly.I can see the hazy reflection of her in the glass, her eyebrows pinched together in pleasure, lips open in a silent moan.

I look down at her legs shaking with a smile."I've got you love. All fucking mine" I groan

I look down, just watching as my cock slides in and out of her swollen pussy.So fucking perfect.I fuck her slow and hard, her whimpers almost echoing through the air."So. Fucking. Deep." She cries out, voice shaky.

"I know baby... you can take it. I'm not done with you yet." I groan, kissing along her shoulder.

Her hair is wet and travels down her back, her whole body flushed as I take her.I know she's exhausted but her hips still move back to grind against me as I thrust inside her.That's it. Take what you need doll.

"You gonna cum for me again doll? I just want to feel your pretty pussy cum around my cock one more time. Can you do that for me?" I say against her ear, holding onto her tightly."God- yes" she whimpers"That's my girl"I bring my hand between her legs, rubbing her clit softly as I push deep inside her pussy, hitting just the right spot.

She nearly collapses in my arms as she cums, her legs going completely weak. I hold her up against me as I grind into her pussy, letting her ride out the orgasm as long as I can.She's so fucking tight I can barely hold on.With a final thrust, I cum inside her sweet pussy, groaning loudly.

I bring her back under the stream of water, cleaning her off as I hold her up in my arms."You okay doll?" I say softly, a bit concerned as I brush the wet strands of hair out of her face."Fucking great" she grins, eyes falling closed.I laugh, turning the water off.

I carry her out the shower, wrapping her up in a towel as I go to lay her down on the bed.Taking it off, I dry her off softly before going to the bathroom to grab her a glass of water.My eyes go over her soft body, noticing the light bruises forming on her hips from my grip, then the red marks around her throat.I frown to myself, worried I got carried away.

As if she could sense my thoughts, she put a hand on my arm, looking up at me."I liked everything you did okay? Don't look at me like that..." she reassures me softly.I smile down at her, kissing her pretty lips.This woman is perfect for me.I don't deserve her.

"You're the best thing that's ever happened to me you know?" I tell her, brushing my thumb over her cheek.She laughs softly, biting her lip."I know"I smirk, lying down as I pull her into my arms.I drag a blanket over her, pressing a kiss to the top of her head."Go to sleep angel. I'll be here when you wake up" I tell her softly

She rests her head against my chest as her eyes fall closed, humming softly.I stroke her hair, playing with the damp curls as she falls asleep.My perfect girl.

# Chapter 27- Hailey

Waking up in Ryder's arms is so much better than I used to imagine. I'm practically laying on top of him, one of his arms hooked tightly around my waist. The other arm is around my hips, his hand squeezing my ass as he notices I'm waking up. "Good morning" I smile softly

He gazes down at me, "Good morning doll" He smirk as he flips us over, pressing a dozen kisses all over my face and jawline until I'm laughing and smiling. "There's my pretty girl"

I grin, shoving his massive body off of me as I sit up, stretching out my sore muscles. As I stand up, Ryder comes behind me, his hands holding my hips. "Sore love?" He asks softly, rubbing his hands over my skin. So concerned... it's cute "I'm completely fine... I'm tougher than you think you know?" I turn around, grinning up at him.

"Is that so?" He muses, tilting my chin up so I'm looking at him. I nod. He leans down to my ear. "Guess that means I'll have to fuck you harder next time" he smirks I practically choke on air.

He laughs, amused as he leaves my room, heading downstairs. "Breakfast doll?" I roll my eyes, following him downstairs. I sit on the counter beside him and wait for my bagel to toast as he makes us some eggs.

"You going into work tonight?" He asks, turning to me. I sigh softly "yeah, I haven't been in the past few days so I need to start working again" I tell him, my legs dangling back and forth off the counter.

"You know I was serious yesterday when I told you that you didn't have to work anymore... I could take care of us doll" he tells me, his hand resting on my thigh. Tempting...

"I don't know... I don't mind my job. It gives me something to do." He nods softly "And I'm much too independent to let you pay for everything in my life." I laugh He frowns softly. Before he can speak, I cut him off.

"What do you do for work anyways? I mean... you spend almost all your time watching me. Well- now with me" I look up at him curiously He stops for a moment, taking a breath.

"You don't need to worry about that... I make enough money for you to have whatever you'd like. Anything." He tells me, rubbing my thigh.

I frown softly, annoyed. "Come on, just tell me." I try and reason "I don't think that's for the best." I roll my eyes. Fucking annoying ass. "God- you watch me constantly and get to know everything about me. It's the least you could fucking tell me." I sigh, looking up at him. "Alright..."

"I'm a bounty hunter. I get paid to find and get rid of people. The scum of the earth." He tells me hesitantly. He looks down at me with a worried expression.

I pause for a moment, my mouth dropping open "Baby I-" I cut him off "I can't believe you're a bounty hunter!" I say in shock "Doll- I swear I" "You are the absolute WORST at being subtle. I'm surprised anyone pays you for this" I tell him and he just freezes. He looks down at me with his lips parted.

"I fucking figured out you were watching me after like a week." I laughHe looks at me, just silent.Then he laughs.A big, chest rumbling laugh I've never seen from him before.I look up at him in confusion as he cups my cheeks, kissing my lips.

"I fucking love you" he tells me, looking down at me in adoration.Holy shit.I don't know what to say.

I mean- I kind of felt like it was obvious given the obsession... but hearing him say it out loud was different.So different.

His fingers brush over my cheeks as he leans down to kiss me again."You don't have to say anything doll, it's okay" he smiles down at me.He just turns back to the eggs, putting them on two plates for us casually.He hands me one with a grin.

I take the plate, setting it aside.I grab him, wrapping my arms around his neck as I look up at him, nervous."I love you" I tell him softly.

The second the words leave my lips, he hoists me up into his arms, the biggest fucking smile on his face.I love him.I can't even help it.

"My girl loves me" he says mesmerizedHe holds me tighter, pressing kisses all over my face and a few on my lips."You love me?" He gets out breathlessly, like he can't believe it.I nod, a big smile on my face.

"God I love you so much. My fucking perfect angel. I love everything about you" he tells me and my heart melts.I can't stop smiling.I've never felt this before.Just so fucking happy.

He picks up the food, sitting down with me in his lap.He holds a bagel with cream cheese in front of my lips, waiting for me to bite.He smiles when I do.

"You feeding me now?" I ask, laughing."Yes, I'm feeding my beautiful girl who loves me." He grins widely.I laugh, rolling my eyes at his childish grin.I love this man.

•••

Ryder's been all over me the rest of the day, constantly having his arms around me.

"No. You can't come in the shower with me" I tell him again as the big man literally sulks.

"Come on doll, let me in" he pleads from the other side of the door.This man is literally begging.

"No! If I let you in with me, you'll end up fucking me..." I explain again. "Exactly" I can fucking feel him smirking from behind the door."I need to get ready for work Ryder- it'll be 10 minutes" I sigh, stepping under the shower.

I hear him mumbling complaints the whole time, making me laugh.After I shower, I get changed into some jeans and a black tank top, pulling my hair into a bun.

He acts fucking deprived when I come back out.So dramatic sometimes I laugh as he kisses me multiple times before finally releasing me from his hold."You look good doll" he grins down at me.He grabs one of my hands, holding it above my head."Give me a spin angel" he say smoothly.

I give in, feeling his eyes all over me as I give him a slow twirl.He licks his lips as the sight."So fucking good" he mumbles"I need to go Ryder" I plead softly"No- we need to go" he smirks, taking his keys out of his pants."I'm driving"

# Chapter 28- Ryder

-------------------------------------------------

She loves me.She loves me.She fucking loves me.

I don't know how this possibly happened but thank fuck it did.I drive her to the bar, my hand resting on her thigh with a grin.This perfect woman loves me.

"I've never seen you smile so much... you're scaring me" I laugh softly."How could I not be smiling when I have you all to myself doll?" I look over at her blushing face.Perfect.

"You know you're actually a huge softie. You look scary but you don't bite..." she tells me, placing her hand over mine."Oh I definitely bite doll." I smirk as she smacks my arm softly, making me laugh.

"I was wondering something for a while..." she starts, peaking my interest."About 2 weeks ago or so, I noticed you didn't come to watch me for 2 days... it just always seemed strange to me" she explains"What, you worried about me doll?" I tease

"No- I just thought it was weird you suddenly stopped watching me... what else were you up to?" She arches a brow at me.Oh.She missed me. I grin.

"Oh I missed watching you too doll, believe me" I say, rubbing her thigh .She sighs, annoyed.I hide a laugh"I was on a job doll... I didn't want to leave you. Promise. Nothing to be jealous about." I smirk."Oh I was not-"I squeeze her thigh harshly, making her stop."Don't lie to me now angel..." I tskShe leans back in her chair giving me a murderous look.It's turning me on.

Once we arrive, I open her door as she rolls her eyes at me, taking my hand.Feisty tonight.

I take a seat down at the bar, watching her.God this reminds me of how things used to be...And now she's all mine.She angrily sets down a drink in front of me, not even saying a word as she runs off to take other orders.That's alright doll. I'll fuck that attitude right out of you later.

After a few hours, she's still ignoring me as I sit there staring at her.So damn pretty.

"You look lonely..." I hear a soft voice to my right.I turn to face some petite woman giving me a flirty smile."I'm not" I say coldly, turning away from her.She plops down on the seat next to me, not getting the fucking message."I could keep you company" she smiles at me, twirling with the straw in her drink.

"I've got a woman to keep me company. Not interested." I tell her, cringing at the way she leans closer."I don't see her..." she smirks playfully as she touches my arm.I pull away, annoyed."I'm-" I get cut off

"Now you see her." I look over to see my girl in front of us, glaring down at the woman beside me.I smile. That's right baby.I'm all yours.

The woman stutters out some stupid nonsense, her lips parted in shock as she steps back from me."I think you should get the fuck out of this bar before something unfortunate happens" Hailey tells her, making the woman visibly tremble.I never thought seeing my woman threaten someone would be such a fuckin turn on.Fuck.

The girl hurries away, and my angel smirks proudly.So fucking hot.

I grab her, pulling her so that she's standing between my spread legs."Give me a kiss doll" I smirk widely.She leans in, and I kiss her passionately. My hands move down to her hips, gripping them firmly as she feels up my arms.She pulls back, and before she can go back to work, I grab her jaw.

I lean in close, bringing my lips to her ear."I'm going to fuck you so fucking hard when we get home. That was so damn hot" I growl lowly, finally releasing her.She blushes, biting her lower lip before she walks back behind the bar.She has a smile on her face as she heads to take more orders, looking back at me.

No more attitude I guess.Looks like she just needed a reminder that I'm all hers.

The next few hours fly by, and I entertain myself by flirting with her the whole time.I just love how she looks all flustered."You gonna scream for me later tonight, huh baby?" I say softly, so that only she can hear me.

Her thighs clench together slightly as she gives me those pretty little fuck me eyes.The second we get home baby.She sighs as she goes back to finish her shift, looking over at me every few minutes.

I patiently wait for everyone to clear out of the bar, watching her get everything cleaned up for closing.Finally, I walk her back to my car, opening the door for her as she slides inside.

I start driving us back to her house, speeding well over the limit.I needed to have my girl all to myself.

"You telling off that woman doll... so fucking hot. I nearly bent you over the bar right there in front of her." I groan softly, my hands tightening around the wheel.

"Yeah?" She smirks, biting her bottom lip."Sexiest thing I've ever fuckin seen" I look over at her, seeing her unbuckle her seatbelt."What are you doing doll- fuck." She reaches over the console, palming my cock over my jeans.

I curse loudly as she starts to undo my belt, my breathing ragged.My dick has been hard since she threatened that chick. All damn night.

My girl licks her lips as she takes out my cock, stroking it as she leans over."Oh fuck doll- look at you" I groan, forcing my eyes to look back up on the road so I don't crash.You're gonna kill us both doll.

I hiss as I fell her warm tongue glide over the head of my cock, tasting the pre cum that's already leaking from the tip.She moans softly at the taste, driving me insane.

I feel her perfect lips wrap around me, sucking softly as she swirls her tongue around the tip."Fuck baby- just like that" I grit out, nearly swerving off the road.

She takes my cock deep into her throat, hollowing her cheeks as she sucks me harder.She starts to bob her head up and down and I feel like my vision is blurring.

"God- fuck your so damn good for me baby. Sucking my cock like a good fucking girl. When I get my hands on you doll-" I groan loudly.

I grip her hair out of her face with one hand, using other to drive quickly back to her place.I'm going to loose my mind.I groan loudly as I approach her house, feeling myself about to cum already.Her mouth just feels so damn good.She's so fucking perfect.I can't help it.

I pull into her driveway, hastily putting the car in park as I lean back. My eyes close as she gags softly on my dick, sucking harder. "Fuck baby- gonna make me cum down your pretty little throat" She moans around my cock at my words and it feels so good it sends me over the edge. I groan loudly as I release into her mouth, gripping her hair harshly.

She glances up at me as she releases my dick with a soft pop from her lips. I swear she looks so fucking hot as she swallows my cum, my dick already starts hardening again. This woman is unbelievable.

I grab her, pulling her onto me as I kiss the fuck out of her. She moans softly into my mouth as I kick my car door open, carrying her inside.

I grip her ass firmly with my hands as I walk through her front door, setting her on the kitchen counter. The bedroom was just too far away.

"I'm going to fucking devour you doll."

# Chapter 29- Hailey

---

I couldn't help myself. The way he was looking at me all night, whispering what he wanted to do to me when we got home...Fuck.

Not to mention the way he didn't give that bitch who was hitting on him a second of fucking attention. Just shooed her away without a second glance. Hot.

I could see the bulge in his jeans when I got in the car, straining against his pants. He was my man. And tonight made that abundantly clear to me for the first time. And I wanted to do something about it.

I quickly unbuckle my seatbelt, leaning over towards him while I drive. He questions me, looking confused before I move to undo his belt, licking my lips.

I slip my hand into his boxers, taking out his cock that's already rock hard for me. Damn. My mouth is watering.

He curses as I stroke him, and I enjoy being the person making him squirm for once.

His grip on the steering wheel tightens as I lick around the head of his cock, swirling around the tip.

I then wrap my lips around him, sucking as I take him into my mouth, teasingly slow.My panties are soaked at the sound of his strained groans, and I know he's struggling to drive right now.But I couldn't care less.

I take him as deep as I can into my throat, noticing as his foot presses the gas pedal to the floor."God- fuck your so damn good for me baby. Sucking my cock like a good fucking girl. When I get my hands on you doll-" he grits out.

His words cause me to moan around his cock, bobbing my head up and down as he speeds back to my place.One of his hands grips my hair tightly as he softly guides me. I hollow out my cheeks, sucking him deeper as he turns into my driveway.

I feel the car come to a halting stop, his grip on my hair tightening as I cont inue."Fuck baby- gonna make me cum down your pretty little throat"God that's so hot.

I keep up my pace, wanting to make him cum more than anything else right now.I get my wish moments later, feeling him release in my mouth, the taste of him filling my senses.

I lean up, looking him in his eyes as I swallow.I wanted him to see me.And the way his eyes turn dark tells me everything I needed to know.I was so fucked.And I was excited.

He grabs me and the next moment I'm out of the car, my legs wrapped around him as he beelines for the house.I whine softly as his hands kneed my ass, kicking the door shut behind him.

I'm speechless as he sets me down on the kitchen counter, looking fucking starved.

"I'm going to fucking devour you doll" he says lowly.Oh god.All I can do is nod softly, awaiting whatever he'll do to me.

He grips the back of my neck, kissing me harshly as his fingers dig into my skin.I moan softly as his lips go down to my neck, marking the skin as he lifts up my shirt.

"So damn sexy" he mumbles before unclasping my bra, kissing and biting along my tits.I hold the back of his head, pulling him closer as I whimper for more.

His hands hastily tug off my jeans and my thong in one go, leaving me bare on the cool countertop."Ryder- please" I bite my lip in anticipation.

He smirks as he kneels down, parting my legs wide.He stares at my pussy, groaning as he pulls me closer.

"So wet and I haven't even touched you baby" he taunts, licking his lips. "You get this wet sucking my cock doll? Hm? Fuck you look so good" he groans softly

I'm squirming in his hold as he finally slips his head between my thighs, licking along my folds slowly."Fuck..." I moan loudly, my head falling back.I was so damn sensitive.My fingers clawed into his hair as he began to eat me out, his tongue gliding over my clit.

"So fucking good doll. I'd drown in you" he mumbles against my pussy, diving in for more.I grip his hair harder, his tongue flicking and sucking my clit in just the right way to make my whither."Ryder" I moan loudlyI feel him groan in appreciation against my pussy, two of his fingers slipping inside me.

I moan out, gasping for air as his fingers curl inside me in sync with his tongue.My legs begin to tremble as the familiar tightness forms in my stomach.

I move my hips greedily against his face, crying out in pleasure as I feel my orgasm coming.

"Oh fuck- yes!" I moan, my body shuttering as my orgasm washes over me. Ryder doesn't relent, going faster as he works me through my high. My eyes roll back as I grind sloppily against his tongue, taking everything I can get. He finally pulls back, licking my cum off his lips with a wicked smirk.

"So damn sweet" he grins He comes between my legs wrapping my legs around his waist as his hard cock rests against my pussy.

"I'm going to fuck you till you're screaming my name baby... and you're gonna love it" he says, gazing darkly over my body. I nod eagerly, and the next thing I know, his dick is buried deep inside me. "Fucking hell doll" he growls, pulling out almost completely before slamming back inside me.

I cry out, gripping onto his shoulders for dear life as my pussy flutters around him. He captured my lips as he fucked me deep and hard, my moans flooding into his mouth.

"So fucking good" I whimper as he drills inside me, hitting spots I wasn't even aware of. His hand comes up to grip one of my breasts, the thumb flicking over my hardened nipple.

"You're all mine. All fucking mine yeah?" He grits out, angling himself deeper inside me. I moan, nodding in agreement as my eyes find his.

"You'll be my fucking wife" Thrust. "You'll wear my ring" Thrust. "And you'll have my last name" Thrust.

Oh my fucking god.

"Nothing can save you from that fate doll. Nothing" he grits out lowly, fucking me straight to heaven.

"Yes- god yes" I cry out, my pussy clenching around his cock as I cum so hard I nearly pass out. "That's right doll, fucking cum for me" he groans, gripping onto my hips as he fucks me through my orgasm. My whole body shakes as his cock fills me over and over. My lips part in a broken scream, my eyes prickling with tears at how good it feels.

He holds my body up to him, kissing me roughly."Feel so damn good around me. Fucking perfect" he groans, his eyes closing in pleasure.I whimper as he continues, my eyes rolling back at the overstimulation.Moments later I feel him cum inside me, his thrusts finally slowing.

"Fucking hell Ryder" I say breathlessly, grinning.He laughs softly, leaning down to kiss me slowly.He hold me closely in his arms before me pulls out, looking down between us.

He stares as our combined release as it leaks out of me, cursing lowly."Fuck- just that sight of you makes me want to cum again" he sighs.His finger coming down to glide over my pussy, rubbing the releases over my folds.My body quivers.

He bites his bottom lip, looking back up at my tired face.He grins softly, grabbing a towel to clean me off before carrying me up to bed.

"Did so fucking good for me doll" he mumbles into my ear, wrapping his arms around me tightly.

"I love you" I say softly against his chest, my eyes closing as I drift off.He kisses my head softly, stroking my back.

"I love you so much more angel"

# Chapter 30- Ryder

I glance angrily over at my phone as it rings for the third time this morning, grumbling. I reluctantly slip my sleeping girl out of my arms, getting up to answer it.

"What the fuck is it?" I whisper, pissed off as I step outside Hailey's bedroom so I don't wake her. "Got a job for you. It's high value and needs to be done quick. I need you to go check it out. ASAP." I recognize the voice of my coordinator.

I sigh, groaning. "I told you I'm busy. Not planning on taking anything over the next few weeks. I have other shit to attend to" I tell him, annoyed.

"Come on. I'll send you the details. It's 30 minutes away from you. Fucking dumb rookie. You won't take even a day." He continues, making my pinch my nose as I think.

"You owe me this Ryder. There's a huge bounty on this mother fucker. In and out." He pleads and I roll my eyes.

"Fine. Send over the info." I groan, regretting this already. I hang up the phone, turning back around to see Hailey in the doorway. Fuck. She doesn't look happy with me.

"You're leaving?" She arches a perfect brow at me, waiting.

"I'm sorry doll. I'll just be gone for a day, at most. Don't give me that look angel..." I sigh softly.I try and reach out for her and she steps back from me, making me frown.

"I don't want you getting hurt. I don't want you to go." She says firmly, standing her ground.I smile softly"Come on doll, you really think I wouldn't come back to you? I'll always make it back to you." I reassure her.She just pushes past me without a word, looking pissed off.Come on angel.

"I have to leave now baby... come on now. Give me a kiss" I say smoothly.She turns around with a fiery look in her eyes, making her so much hotter."Fuck you" she spits outI grab her, pulling her lips to mine as I steal the kiss from her.She huffs, pushing me off her.Don't be mad at me doll.I can't take it.

"I'll see you soon angel" I call out to her, walking out the door.She'll come around.

I know she has work tonight so at least she won't be bored all alone at home.She might even like some alone time since I haven't left her side in days.

I sigh as I hop into my car, dropping by my place to pick up a few things before heading to the job.

I set up my things, staking out this man's rental cabin in the woods.Fucking piece of shit beat his girlfriend so bad she ended up in the hospital.I'd make sure his death was extra painful.

The clock ticked by as I waited, and I watched on the cameras as my girl left for work.I'm sorry I'm not there love.I sigh, the air getting cooler as the sun sets.

I keep my eyes trained on the windows, looking for anything. And my girl said I was such a terrible stalker.

•••

It's hours later and I watch as Hailey makes it back home from work, wishing I was there to hold her in my arms. At least with this job I'd be set for a long time. No more favors to owe. I'd take a break and just be with her.

I lean back in my car, my eyes noticing a slight shadow in the windows. That's it. Just show me your face.

I worry nothing else will come, but then about an hour later, I see him slip out onto the porch to grab more firewood. Got you.

I silently get out of my car, making my way there just in time before he can close the door behind him. He looks back at me, eyes widening as he makes a run for it. Sick fucking bastard. I chase him through the cabin, quickly cornering him. Fucking pathetic.

"No! Please- I haven't done anything!" He gasps out, pleading with me. I grip onto his shirt, lifting him up so that he's looking right into my eyes. "You know what I fucking hate?" I grit lowly. He shakes his head, trembling. "A fucking miserable little shit who puts his hands on a woman." I spit at him.

I knee him in the gut, letting him drop to his knees before I bang his head against the wall.

Still conscious. He'll feel what I do to him.

I grab a hunting knife from my back pocket, sinking it into his thigh as he screams like a little bitch. "You're the fucking worst kind of human." I look down at him, watching him bleed. I take the knife out, sticking it into his gut, twisting. The man cries out in agony, sobbing before he blacks out. No more fun. Shame.

I take out the knife, leaving him to bleed to death as I walk out the door. I call my guy, letting him know the job's done as I get into my car. Back to my girl.

I stop at my place for a few minutes, washing that disgusting prick off me and changing before I get to her.

She's fast asleep when I come in, looking so calm and sweet compared to how she was earlier. I grin widely as I lie down next to her, pulling her into my arms softly. So damn pretty. She doesn't wake up, just nuzzles into my chest with a sleepy sigh. Fucking perfect.

I close my eyes, hoping that she's come around and forgiven me for leaving. I told her I'd come back to her. Always.

I feel over her soft skin as I let out a satisfied hum, drifting off to sleep myself. I'd have her back smiling in my arms tomorrow.

# Chapter 31- Hailey

Oh hell fucking no.

The second I wake up in his arms I thrash out of his grip, hitting him against his chest angrily.

"What the fuck-" he groans softly, waking up."You think you get to have me all cuddled up in your arms? Fuck off Ryder." I say annoyed, climbing out of bed.Yes I know I'm being petty.But he doesn't get to follow me everywhere, telling me what to do and then ignore me when I say something.I was still angry.

"Doll... come on. Come back and talk to me." He sighs, reaching out for me.I step away from him, rolling my eyes."You just fucking left without a care. I told you I didn't want you to go..." I tell him.

"Please love... what do I have to do for you to forgive me. I just wanna touch you doll. Give me something" he pleads.An idea pops into my head."You really want me to forgive you?" I turn back to face him and he smiles.Oh you have no idea what's coming.

"Anything doll. Please forgive me" he reaches out for me, thinking I'm getting over it.Wrong."Okay then... I'll be right back" I grin, walking into my closet.I come back out, 2 belts in my hand.Oh this is going to be so much fun.

He raises an eyebrow at me as I crawl to him on the bed with a seductive smile.I take one of his hands, strapping it to my headboard with the belt."Ah... you wanna be in control baby? Fuck me while I can't touch you?" He smirks up at me."Mmhm" I smile, tightening the belt on his other wrist.That should hold him.

I take my time, straddling him as I let my hands feel up his chest.He groans softly as I grind against him, feeling his cock get hard beneath me.His arms flex as he tries to fight against the restraints.Perfect.Right where I want him.

"Come on doll- stop teasing" he hisses lowly, lifting his hips up to press against me.I bite my lip, getting off his lap before moving to stand in front of the bed.He looks over me hungrily, telling me to come back to him.

"Oh baby, but I have something special planned for you" I grin.I begin to slowly strip out of the clothes I was sleeping in.I glide the oversized shirt over my head, loving the way his eyes darken and his muscles tense.

I then unclasp my bra, letting the straps slowly fall down my shoulders before dropping to the floor."Fuck doll" he groans, the bulge in his sweatpants obvious.I pay him no mind as I turn around, bending over as I drag the panties I was wearing down my legs.

I can hear him cursing, the leather belts pulling against the headboard as he tries to get free.Not so soon baby.

I turn around, giving him a view of my completely bare body as I smirk widely.

"This isn't funny doll." He says lowly, looking over at me like he's starved. "Oh- I'm not trying to be funny" I turn around, dragging a chair in front of the bed before sitting back in it. He's looking at me like he wants to fucking kill me, and I don't know if I should run or be turned on. But that's not my problem right now.

"I wanted to give you a show Ryder... one you've seen before, but closer up." I smile, planting my feet on the edge of the bed. I spread my legs wide, letting him see my soaking wet pussy. He growls deeply, pulling against the belts.

I tsk. "Oh don't hurt yourself... just sit back and enjoy love" I tease, grasping my breasts in my hands.

I let out a soft whine as my fingers brush over my hardened nipples, arching my back up. "Angel..." he says lowly. Ooh. I'm scared.

One of my hands slips down my stomach, my fingers grazing up my slit slowly. I let out a soft moan as I begin to circle around my clit, looking up into his furious eyes. "God- If you could feel how wet I am" I gasp softly.

I bite my lip as his skin starts to get flushed and angry, the veins in his arms prominent as he fights against the restraints. "You don't wanna do this doll." He warns, his eyes burning into my skin.

I just work my fingers faster, moaning as I use my free hand to pinch one of my nipples. The whole bed shifts as he tries to thrash against the belts. I might have to keep him tied up forever. God help me when I finally undo those belts.

I gasp out softly as I slip a finger into my entrance, working it in and out before adding a second. This is turning me on so much. The way he's looking at me... anger radiating off of him. The power I feel, knowing he can't touch me no matter how badly he wants to...I feel drunk on pleasure and control.

Most of all, the part of me that's excited to see what he'll do to me when I get the balls to untie him. The thought of it makes me shiver.

I work my fingers in and out faster, curling them up like Ryder does. His fingers feel so much better.

I moan loudly, glancing up as him with my 'fuck me' eyes. I feel my body begin to shutter as my orgasm approaches. "Oh my god- Ryder" I moan loudly, feeling him jerk against the bed.

My eyes fall closed as my head leans back in ecstasy. Ryder curses loudly as his eyes are glued on my fingers, working in and out of my dripping entrance. My orgasm overcomes me, my back arching against the chair as I keep going, prolonging it as long as I can.

I eventually slow down, my eyes meeting his furious ones as my fingers slip out of me. "You're gonna regret that doll" he says, gripping the headboard tightly.

I smile, bringing my fingers to my lips before sucking my release off them slowly. "Mmm. You were right. I do taste addictive" I smirk widely.

He groans, pulling against the restraints tightly as I laugh. "Hm, and what are you gonna do when you have to untie me huh?" He smirks devilishly, eying me up.

"Maybe I won't release you then... just keep you tied up. Never let you have a taste of my sweet pussy again-"

Snap.

I look up with wide eyes as he broke one hand free. He smirks like predator that just found an injured lamb. Oh fuck.

I jump up out of my seat, hearing the other belt snap against his strength .Oh fuck oh fuck oh fuck.

As I scramble to the door, I feel his large arms wrap around me, pulling me back.

"Got you now doll."

# Chapter 32- Ryder

I angrily tug against the headboard, wanting nothing more than to break it off.

"Hm, and what are you going to do when you have to untie me huh?" I ask, smirking as I see Hailey physically shiver.

She's acting cocky, but I can tell she's realizing the position she's in now.

"Maybe I won't release you then... just keep you tied up. Never let you have a taste of my sweet pussy again-"The mere thought of not getting a taste of her gave me a second wave of anger.

Snap.

I look over, seeing my right hand now free.Ohh you're in for it now doll.I smirk widely at her, her face going pale as her expression turns from confidence to panic.

I'm easily able to break the other wrist free with both hands, and she's already running for the door.Not so fast angel.

I quickly get off the bed, wrapping my arms around her tightly just before she can get away.

"Got you now doll" I smirk widely, picking her up as she kicks and pleads.She's babbling breathless apologies as I bring her back over to the chair she sat in.

"And how did you think this was going to play out for you doll? Didn't use that pretty brain of yours huh?"

I set her squirming body down on the floor in front of me.She's a vulnerable mess as sit back in the chair, looking over her perfect body all exposed to me.Not so fun now angel.

Grabbing her, I pull her down, putting her body so that she's bent over my lap.She whines softly, and I know she can feel the anger radiating off me.

"I'm sorry- please I-"She's cut off as I smack her ass hard, causing a soft whimper to leave her lips.

"You're not sorry doll. You knew exactly what you were fucking doing." I grit out, spanking the other cheek as she yelps softly.

I sigh, admiring the red handprints left on her ass.

"You don't get to pull away from me, cause I will always catch you. You hear that? Always." I smack her ass for the third time, and she moans out.

"You like that angel? Did you just want all my attention on you baby?" I tease, rubbing over her ass softly.I slowly trace up the back of her thighs, grinning as she squirms against my lap.

"No- I was fucking mad at you" she huff softly

I tsk at her, grinning."I bet if I spread your pretty thighs you'd be fucking dripping for me"

She mumbles in protest, biting her lip as I spread her thighs a bit. Fucking soaked. I smirk, as bring my fingers to her drenched folds, grazing over them lightly,

"Such a little brat today" I mumble. Suddenly, I thrust two fingers inside her, loving the way she moans out in surprise.

I don't give her any time to think before I start fucking her with my fingers, feeling her tight little pussy clench around them.

"You thought you could deny me what's mine?" I ask, smacking her ass again.

"No- oh god" she cries softly, moaning. I move my fingers faster, my ego growing at the way she's withering beneath me. "Feels good hm? I just know all the spots your pretty fingers can't seem to hit right?"

"Yes- I'm sorry- please" she gasps out, and I can feel how she's about to cum.

So I stop.

She cries out in frustration, mumbling about how sorry she is. "Why don't you get on your knees and show me how sorry you are?"

I look down at her, watching as she slowly moves off my lap, sinking to her knees.

She looks up at me as she cautiously moves to take out my cock, licking her lips. "You sorry angel?" I ask her in a condescending tone. She nods, leaning down as she licks over the head of my cock. I sigh softly, my fingers threading into her scalp as I grip her hair.

I feel her mouth wrap around the tip, bobbing her head up and down slowly. "Look at me" I tell her, and her eyes flash up to meet mine. "That's it. Maybe I just need to keep this pretty mouth full till you learn not to test me." I groan softly.

I push her head down further until I feel her gag.She was going to learn that she was mine.

I start moving her head up and down faster, my dick pushing down her throat as I bottom out."So eager to please" I tell her, smirking.

She nods softly, sucking harder as her eyes begin to water.I only grip her hair harder, groaning at the feeling.She keeps her eyes on me even as tears begin to fall down her soft cheeks.Looks so fuckin pretty and helpless in front of me.

I pull her head back, watching with a smirk as she breathes heavily."You have a fucking problem, you talk with me about it. Cause I won't have you walking away from me. Never" I tell her, my thumb brushing over her swollen lips.

She nods softly, looking up at me with wide eyes.I pick her up, hearing her gasp as I bend her over the bed."Now you're going to let me fuck my pussy, and you're going to love every single second" I tell her, gripping her hips."Yes sir" she mumbles softly against the mattress.Not wasting another moment, I push inside her, groaning at how good she feels wrapped around me.

"You don't get to walk away from me. This." I groan out."I won't- I'm not" she moans, turning her head back so she can look at me.I move one of my hands to grip her jaw, holding her gaze as I fuck her relentlessly.

She cries out as I go deeper, gripping the sheets beneath her. I release her jaw, letting her fall down into the mattress as I drill inside her.I needed to claim every fucking inch of her.

I pull her hips back to meet each of my thrusts, her moans echoing off the walls,"You gonna cum on my cock doll? Can't even help yourself" I groan, feeling her walls tighten around me.

"Ryder-" she cries out as her body shakes.Her skin glistens with sweat as I keep my pace, feeling her cum for me.Fucking heaven"That's it baby" I grin, basking in the feeling of her getting impossibly tighter around me.

I give into the feeling, cumming with her as my thrusts begin to slow down.I stay there for a few moments, silent as the both of us catch our breath.Once I finally pull out of her, she lies back, looking up at me nervously.

I look down at her,"Don't move. We're not done here"

# Chapter 33- Hailey

I wait nervously for Ryder to return, not sure what to expect. I knew he wouldn't truly hurt me. Even when he's angry. But still.

My body was so spent I wasn't sure if I could even handle more. But I knew I'd let him take what he needed from me.

I lean up a bit as he returns to the room, his expression unreadable. "I'm sorry I-" I begin "Stop." I shut my mouth, and he leans over me, spreading my legs. I then feel a warm washcloth cleaning our release off of me slowly. I look up at him, letting out a soft breath.

Once I'm cleaned up, he slips on some boxers and grabs my lotion off the dresser. Still silent, he takes time to rub the lotion in all over my body, massaging my sore muscles. He even turns me over, rubbing some into my ass that's still imprinted with his hand.

I don't know what to do, I've never seen him so impassive.

After another few minutes, he grabs his shirt off the floor, putting it on over my head. The soft material feels nice against my skin and it smells like him.

He sits down on the bed, pulling me onto his lap. I force myself to keep quiet even though all I want is to ask what he's doing.

He just sits there looking over my face, analyzing every little detail.

"I can't handle not having you" he says softly. "I know."

"Talk to me. Please. Why did me leaving upset you so much?" He asks, brushing the hair out of my face.

"I asked you not to go and you didn't even care to talk to me about it. You just left." I frown softly

"I knew I'd be okay. I knew that there was nothing to worry about." Ryder tells me

"But you don't understand how I'd feel. I was worried. You didn't even care what I had to say about it. You had already decided." I explain

"I'm sorry, I never what you to feel like I don't care about what you think. Your opinion is all I fucking care about. I just wanted to get done so I'd be back to you sooner. I'm sorry angel." He tells me, cupping my face gently.

"I'm so fuckin sorry you had to worry about me. And I'm an idiot for not taking your words seriously. Fuck- and the way I just treated you... I lost my composure." He sighs, looking down at me with such regret.

I shake my head softly, "I need it too. I need you to take me like you need me more than anything. I need to feel the way you have complete control over me, because I trust you. You make me feel wanted. Loved."

He looks down at me with a soft smile, kissing me gently. "You're too damn perfect. I fucking love you with my entire being."

"I love you too" I relax as he pulls me closer into him, wrapping his arms around me.

"I want to spend the day with you. Take you shopping so I can fucking spoil you and then take you out to dinner tonight. Treat my girl exactly how you deserve." He tells me, kissing my head.

"You really know how to make a girl feel special" I laugh softly.

He pulls back, kissing my lips long and slow."Because you are special."I grin widely."I'll go get ready"

•••

Ryder opens the door for me, offering his hand for me to take."Any store you want to go into, fucking anything you want doll." He squeezes my hand, leading us down the streets.

"You don't need to buy me a bunch of shit, I'm happy just with you" He stops and turn to face me, leaning down to my ear."Fucking nothing would make me happier than spending my money on you. I don't even want you to think about it. You want it, it's yours."

Well... if it'll make him happy...

I nod softly and he grins, following me as I head into the first store.There's dozens of beautiful dresses on display and I walk around the store in awe.I don't even know where I'd wear them but they're too gorgeous to not look.

One in the corner catches my attention, It's a beautiful dark green color, completely backless with a long slit.I run my fingers over the silky material, admiring it.

"Go try it on" Ryder says, coming up behind me."I don't even have anywhere to wear it" I tell him, rolling my eyes.

"Says who? Go try it on. I picked out a few others you can try too if you like them" he grins, handing me a few more dresses before leading me back into the fitting rooms.

He sits back in a chair outside as he waits for me to try them on."Come out and show me doll" he calls out, making me laugh.

I try on his picks first, and every time I come out and show him, he makes me do a spin as he showers me in compliments.I look down at the price tag of the one I'm wearing, my eyes widening."Ryder- these are insane. I don't even need them" I try and reason with them.

"It's worth whatever it costs to even just see you in it. You look so damn good doll." He grins, eyeing me up and down."last one" I tell him, heading back into the room to try on the green silk one I picked out.

I smile as I look at myself in the mirror. The dress hugs my body perfectly, showing off my toned back and one of my long legs.I step out of the room, walking over to Ryder.

He smirks, motioning for me to spin as he looks over every inch of me."F ucking stunning. Too good to even be real" he tells me, making me blush.

"Go change before I fuck you right here" he says dead serious, and I quickly go back into the room, hearing him curse to himself.So whipped.

When I come back out, he grabs all the dresses and takes them up to the front despite me telling him I don't need them."Just let me. If you complain about me paying for things one more time I'll buy the whole damn store." He whispered to me, grabbing the bags.

I nod softly, letting him lead me out towards the other shops.Many hours later, Ryder's arms are stacked with shopping bags, buying literally anything I like.Dresses, shoes, workout sets, perfume…It's all so much.But I've never seen him smile so much.

"Anywhere else doll?" He turns to me with a grin.I look over and see a lingerie store across the street."You think you could pick out a few things for me?" I smile up at him as he follows my gaze to the store."There?" I nod and he smirks widely."Anything for you pretty girl" he grins, practically pulling me along with him as he walks over there.

"I'll wait over here with the bags. Surprise me." I tell him once we get into the store.I sit down in a nearby chair, scrolling through my phone as he eagerly walks through the store, picking out things.

He eventually comes back to me with a large bag and a big smile.Looks like he enjoyed himself.

"Ready to go home?" He asks

"Definitely."

# Chapter 34- Ryder

I never liked shopping until it came to spending my money all on my perfect angel. I'd give her my card and let her swipe it all day long if she wanted. But we had other plans to get to.

Once we got back, I brought her bags upstairs and set out that green dress for her tonight. She just looks so fucking good in it. I kiss her pretty lips, telling her how fucking in love with her I was. "I'll be back in an hour to pick you up, ok love?"

She smiles and heads to the bathroom to get herself ready and I drive back to my place.

I shower and get ready, putting on a black suit and some cologne. Needed to look good for my angel tonight.

When I drive back over to her house, I just let myself in with my spare key. "Ryder?" She calls out from upstairs.

"It's just me doll" I grin, heading upstairs to her. I just couldn't wait to see her. When I walk in her room, I just stop and stare at her. She's finishing up putting in some gold earrings, and she looks back at me with a smile. "I'm almost done" "Take your time" I breathe out, taking her in.

She's wearing the green dress I got her earlier and heels that make her legs look even longer.Her hair is pulled up in an elegant bun and she has a bit of makeup on that makes her pretty eyes pop.She grabs a clutch off her dresser, coming over to me.

"What?" She stops in front of me, confused.

"You're the most beautiful thing I've ever fucking seen" I tell her truthfully, looking over her once more.Her face softens and a beautiful smile forms on her lips.God, you're going to kill me baby.

I take her hand, my eyes staying on her the whole time as I walk her out to my car, opening the door for her.

•••

"You're supposed to keep your eyes on the road you know" she tells me as we step inside the restaurant.

"Impossible when you're right next to me looking like that" I grin, sitting down at our table.Had to pull a few strings to get in tonight but it was well worth it.I knew she loved Italian.

The waitress came over and took our orders, the soft lighting of the restaurant making it feel that much more romantic.

"This is amazing Ryder" she looks around with a smile

"I'd do anything for you Angel" I grin, taking her hand in mine.

"You ever wonder what would've happened if that guy didn't break into my house?" She asks me.

I think about it for a few moments, unsure."I probably would've just continued watching you, walking you out to your car until I grew the balls to ask you out finally" I laugh softly, remembering.

"Well... you did kiss me that one night, so I guess you made a move finally." She laughs, biting down on her lower lip.

"I was just too worried about messing it up with you. I knew you were fucking perfect and I didn't want to ruin anything." "I even put a nail in your tire once just so that I'd have an excuse to be around you longer" I admit, laughing.

"Yeah I kind of figured that out..." she smirks"And by the way... I learned how to change a tire when I was 12. Just wanted to let you do it for me... you seemed so proud of yourself." She teases and I raise an eyebrow at her.

"Maybe it's for the best that everything happened this way... now I have you all to myself." I smile, kissing her hand softly.

•••

Our food comes and I can't wipe through smile off my face the entire time.I just loved being here with her.

As we're finishing up, and old buddy of mine recognizes me and came up to me and my girl.

"Ryder? That you man?" He grinsI laugh, "Good to see you Sal""Love, this is Sal, I used to work with him in Chicago. Sal, this is my wife Hailey" I tell him, watching my girl nearly choke on her drink.

Sal extends a hand to her, "Nice to meet you honey. Glad Ryder found himself a beautiful woman." he grins at her.

I hit his shoulder for him to back off.He puts his hands up in the air, grinning."Alright- I got it. Hands off." He laughs, turning back to me.

"We're just heading out but it was good to see you again. Angel?" I reach out my hand for her and she takes it, letting me lead her back out to the car.

"Your wife?" She turns to me, raising a brow. I just smile. "I like the sound of that doll." I wink at her, opening the car door.

"You do know I'm not your wife right?" She laughs, wiggling her ring finger at me. "Not yet. But I've had a ring for you since the first week I saw you doll... just waiting on you" I tell her. Her lips part open for a moment.

"You're insane..." she mumbles, sitting back as I drive. "Only for you baby" I smirk, resting my hand on her thigh. "You don't even know me!" "Oh I know you doll..." I squeeze her thigh teasingly.

"I could take you to my place if you'd like... you could see the ring." I smirk, seeing her bite her lip out of the corner of my eye. "I've never been to your place before." She turns to me, excited. "Nothing special, I just got it so I'd have somewhere close to you." I explain to her and she laughs. "You got a whole apartment so you could spy on me? Seriously?"

"Needed somewhere to stay when I wasn't watching over you" I grin, pulling up to my building.

•••

I follow as she looks around my place carefully, studying everything.

"Not very homey... i wasn't here very much of the time. Had something much more important to do." I grin, following close behind her. "And now I'm rarely ever here. Just can't stand being away from you." I tease, wrapping my arms around her.

"You could just bring your things to my place... I mean- it would probably just be easier for you. Or not- I just was thinking" she rambles on, making me laugh. "You want me to come live with you doll?" I ask her with a grin, turning her so I can see her blushing face. Fucking perfect. "You basically already do you big caveman" she shoves me away grinning.

I laugh, catching her hand before she can pull away, "I'd love to come live with you doll. I love fucking anything with you."

# Chapter 35- Hailey

Ryder wraps his arms around me in a suffocating hug."Ryder- my god let me go" I laugh softly

He loosens his grip, still holding me flush against him."You're my fucking world" he smiles down at me before pulling me in for a kiss.I melt into his touch, his lips soft and warm as I wrap my hands around his neck.

"And you're going to be my wife, and I'll fucking worship you till the day I die. That's all I want" He tells me, kissing me again.

"I love you." I tell him, so overwhelmed by his words."Let me be your husband. Let me take care of you. Fuck- just let me put a ring on your finger so that I can show everyone that you're all mine."

He looks down at me with so much adoration and love, holding my face gently.I can't believe I'm doing this.

"Okay" I look up at him nodding, my eyes watering as a massive smile breaks out on his face.The next second he picks me up in his arms, spinning me around before kissing the fuck out of me."I'll never stop falling more and more in love with you. Fucking made for me." He tells me, setting me down."Don't move." He grins, running off into the other room. I stand there, laughing as he runs back to me, kneeling down.

"Mrs. Fallon sounds fucking perfect doesn't it?" He smirks, taking out a gorgeous engagement ring."You really had a ring already... you're fucking insane and I love you more because of it" I grin widely as he slides the ring onto my finger.

"I thought you couldn't possibly get better- but you with my ring on your finger? Better than perfect." He smirks, kissing my hand as he gets up.

"Now let's get you home. I want to fuck my wife with nothing else but that ring on your finger." He whispers lowly, making my cheeks heat up at the thought.

•••

I laugh as he picks me up bridal style and carries me into the house."You're supposed to do that after we get married you know?" I tell him.

"I'll carry you wherever I damn please doll." He smirks taking us upstairs. I roll my eyes, grinning as he sets me down on the bed. He kneels down in front of me, taking off my heels and tossing them aside.

He stands back up, offering his hand for me to stand up. He comes behind me, leaning down to my ear."Did I tell you how fucking stunning you look in this dress?" He murmurs against my neck."Once or twice." I grin.

He slowly drags down the zipper along the side before letting it fall to the floor."Even better without it." He grins, his hand sliding up the sides of my body as I lean back against him. His hands come around to cup my tits, his thumbs brushing over my nipples.

"Ryder-" I whine softly."Hmm what does my pretty wife want? Tell me angel." He muses, kissing along my shoulder."Please- just do something." I get out impatiently, pushing my ass back against him.

"Whatever my pretty girl wants." He smiled lying me back on the bed.He takes his time kissing up my stomach, his tongue dragging between my breasts as i whimper for him.

He slides my panties down my legs slowly, spreading them."Fucking divine" he mumbles, wrapping his arms around my thighs, his hands griping my hips tightly.

I watch as his tongue drags up my slit, one of my hands making its way into his hair.He groans against my pussy, flattening his tongue out as he glides over my folds.He looks like he's enjoying this even more than me.

I moan softly as he flicks over my clit, circling around it before sucking softly."Oh fuck- Ryder" I moan, gripping his hair tighter.I can feel him grin against my pussy before his mouth covers me completely, licking and sucking like his life depends on it.

My moans get louder as I grind myself against his face, feeling my orgasm approaching."Please- don't stop" I beg breathlessly, my head falling back. His fingers dig into my hips as his tongue works faster."Oh my god-" I cry out, squirming against his grip as my orgasm hit me.It all felt like too much but he didn't stop. His grip wouldn't let me pull away.

He just continued to devour me until he got every last drop, finally releasing me.He looks up at me with a wide smirk."You look so fucking good like this. Cumming all over my face" he groans, licking his lips.

He leans up, getting on top of me.He threads his fingers in mine, pinning them on either side of my head.He glances over at my left hand, grinning at the sight of the big diamond on my finger.

"You belong to me Angel. All mine. Always." He tells me, making my whimper. God that's so hot. He leans down to kiss me, and I can still taste myself on his tongue as I moan into his mouth.

"Every inch of you is so god damn perfect. So responsive for me." He grins down at me. I bite my lip as I glide my fingers under his shirt, taking it off. I wanted to see him.

He takes both of my hands in his, pressing them to his chest so that I can feel over the hard ridges and dips of his muscles. "That's it baby, all yours" he tells me, bringing my thighs to wrap around him.

I feel his hard length pressing up against me and I can't take it anymore. "I need you inside me- please" I beg softly, looking up at you.

"Of course Angel" he smirks, lining up with my entrance. "You know what they say... Happy wife" I choke out a moan as he thrusts into me in one go, bottoming out inside me. "Happy fucking life" he groans out deeply.

My lips part open as he fucks me nice and deep, moaning with every hard thrust. He takes both my hands in one of his, pinning them above me as his other hand grips my jaw, making me look at him. "Fuck- taking me so well. Just like that" he groans, pounding into me harder.

This is what I need. All I need is him.

His thumb brushes over my lips and I part them, letting him into my mouth. He groans loudly as I suck, looking down at me with dark eyes. "Such a pretty little vixen" he smirks, his thumb leaving my mouth with a pop.

"Let me hear you baby. Feels so fucking good" he grits out, sucking and biting along my neck and shoulder. I moan loudly as he hits deep inside me over and over again. "Ryder- oh fuck- please!" I cry out, my eyes rolling back at the intensity.

"Such a perfect mess for me... cum on my cock like the good fucking girl you are." He groans, angling himself impossibly deeper.My whole body stutters as he fucks me straight into another orgasm, my moans filling the room.

"That's it- fuck doll... so fuckin good" he groans loudly, lifting my hips off the bed as he thrusts into me mercilessly.

"Oh god-" I cry out my vision blurring at how good I was feeling.I feel like I might pass out when he finally cums inside me, feeling so unbelievably full.He slows down, smirking down at me as he rubs over my thighs softly.He leans down to kiss my lips, holding me close.

"Happy wife?" He asks with a grin "Very happy wife."

..............